A Vampire's Fight

FATE'S CHRONICLES
BOOK FIVE

RHIANNON FUTCH

Ebook ISBN: 978-1-955749-00-8

Print ISBN: 978-1-955749-26-8

Cover by sunsetrosebooks.com

Editing by V. Editing Services

Contents

Chapter 1	1
Chapter 2	5
Chapter 3	8
Chapter 4	13
Chapter 5	19
Chapter 6	23
Chapter 7	27
Chapter 8	38
Chapter 9	43
Chapter 10	50
Chapter 11	54
Chapter 12	57
Chapter 13	61
Chapter 14	69
Chapter 15	73
Chapter 16	84
Chapter 17	90
Chapter 18	102
Chapter 19	120
Chapter 20	134
Chapter 21	144
Mercy of the Vampire King	149
A Free Story for You!	151
Fated for Halloween preview	153
Epilogue	162
About the Author	167
Also by Rhiannon Futch	169

One

Natasha

I felt Billy get out of bed a few minutes ago but I refused to wake up. I don't want to wake up and face a world that Grams doesn't exist in yet. I know when I open my eyes I will see all her things stacked in my room and I just can't. I hear Billy coming back and I leave my eyes closed. I smell the coffee when he opens the door. No. I won't open my eyes just for coffee. I hear him walk over and feel the bed sink a little as he seats himself.

"Come on love, open your eyes. I know you're awake. Face the day and make her proud." He knows just what to say, the bastard.

Opening my eyes and keeping them focused on him I sit up and reach for the coffee. One sip and I feel just a little stronger. Maybe I can do this. Letting my eyes stray around the room I notice different little trinkets, various things that hung on her walls or lived in baskets throughout her home. Her books, stacked everywhere. Then I see her jewelry box, humming with energy. The jewelry box that my mother thought she took home with her and is now very upset about. I turn my eyes back to Billy, "I don't want to believe she's gone."

"I know. I don't either." He puts his hand on my leg and gives it a squeeze as his pocket starts vibrating.

Looking at his pocket I ask him, "Is that your phone or did you learn a new trick?"

He chuckles, "No new tricks and not my phone, it's yours."

I grimace and take a healthy swig of my coffee, "All right. Give it to me."

He passes it over and I hold it up to unlock it, holy Hera. There are over a hundred messages! The phone unlocked I pull up the notifications and give it a Price is Right spin on the wheel to get to the beginning. They are all from my mother. She is mad as hell that the box she took was not the actual jewelry box. "Babe, come sit next to me and look at these messages. They are all from my mom."

He scoots himself up to sit next to me and read along. Some of the things she calls me, I can hardly believe my mother would say something like this. Billy frowns, "Maybe we shouldn't read all of this right now. I mean, you just woke up. I should have left it downstairs."

"No, better I see it now. Get all the bad out of the way

first thing. Good news, she doesn't seem to be driving over here yet. I haven't given her the address but I won't delude myself that she couldn't find us if she wanted to."

Billy slips an arm around my shoulders, "We have a great barrier around the place, your mom couldn't get in unless we let her."

"I know. I guess I need to get to work. I have a lot to learn and do. I'm not even sure how to wrap my head around it all yet."

"Maybe start with a shower? Clear your mind. Maybe you should resign from the job with Fate? I think someone here could step into your role, take care of the foundation and be Fate's right hand."

Nodding I say, "Ajah could. Or her and Ryna if they chose. But I'm not giving that up. Grams told me that I needed to keep my life outside of being a protector. She said it wouldn't be easy but it would be worth it. She also said that my protector duties would be made much easier by the fact that I have a whole goddess on my side. And, all the research I do with Fate is part of it too, so it all works together."

He nods, "I thought you would feel that way but I wanted to bring it up in case you might feel differently. I am here to support you wherever you take us."

Tipping the cup up I drain the rest of the coffee. Passing him the mug to set on the nightstand I crawl across the bed to hop off the other side and head for the shower. I have to weave my way around piles of things and I pause at the bathroom door to look back at him, "I think today will be for figuring out where to put all these things."

He laughs as I step into the bathroom and start the shower.

Two

FATE

Drifting back to consciousness I am warm and cozy, my limbs tangled up with Devon's and Charles, the comforting weight of Trust and Kindness near my feet. I can't believe how much my life has changed in such a short time. Not long ago I was a widow just trying to stay away from being hurt again. I hadn't even faced how abusive Charlie had been. Now, I am a goddess. I met my birth parents. I have two amazing lovers that work to outdo each other sexually. And I light up like fireworks when I have an orgasm. I sigh in contentment and snuggle in to this cuddle puddle. The guys stir and move in a little closer, I feel the weight of the dogs disappear. Suddenly I have hardness pressing in at me from both sides. What a beautiful life I have fallen into!

We kiss a little before my need for coffee kicks in. Charles laughs and heads for the kitchen. Devon and I cuddle till he gets back. He walks back in minutes later, "Maria had the tray waiting for me."

I sit up eagerly while Devon sighs dramatically, "Tossed aside like old news for coffee." Ignoring him I reach for the tray as Charles draws near, he passes it over before climbing back into bed while I hold the tray steady. We all arrange ourselves with our backs to the headboard before we each delight in the gloriousness that is Maria's coffee.

After some silence and coffee we are all feeling more alive. Devon looks over at us and says, "What are we going to do about Natasha's parents?"

I groan, "We are going to follow her lead. I am more concerned with what is coming next from Demeter and Pru. It feels like they are both planning something and none of it good for me."

Charles adds his thoughts, "As much as I hate to say it, we probably need to go train some more. The stuff your dad puts us through is much more challenging than any obstacle course we could create up here and those dogs are ridiculously fast. Maybe we should see about taking everyone down with us? They could benefit from the training like the rest of us."

Devon chuckles, "Might help us get less drooled on too."

"That had definitely crossed my mind."

Laughing I say, "You have a point. But we have to get permission first. That is their realm. Pretty sure if we take someone down that doesn't have permission they die."

"Hmm," Charles sips his coffee, "I suppose that would be inconvenient."

Devon rolls his eyes, "Inconvenient. I am getting in the shower. Fate, as always, you are welcome to join." He sets his cup on the table and gets out of bed, sautering across the room naked and sexy as hell with his sepia skin and those thighs! Ooo! That butt!

Charles nudges me with an elbow, "Feeling a little ignored over here."

I laugh, "Aw, poor thing. He is just as distracting as you are. It's a wonder I can get anything done these days."

"Well," he takes my cup and sets it with his on the other table, "speaking of getting done, how about it?"

Giggling I push him back and climb on top of him. He growls, "Yes!" as I rub my slit along his length. Reaching the tip I rock my hips just so and he lines up with my entrance. I press down just enough to get the head in and I sit up straight, leaving all that space between our bodies as I begin to rotate my hips, making small circles on the head of his cock. He moans and grips my hips tightly, I drop an inch. He sucks air as I raise back up. I tease him a few minutes longer before I ride us both to completion. Leaving him laying spent on the bed I give him a kiss as I head for Devon in the shower.

Three

After the excellent morning sex and hot shower to finish waking me up, I head downstairs to work in the dining room. Memré joins me not long after.

"Have you seen Natasha this morning?" I ask as I browse office furniture online.

"Nope, I saw Billy wander through with coffee. She is probably taking it slow this morning."

"Good. She should, her mom is pretty extra right now. A lot of the work will get so much easier once we have office furniture anyway. Got a chair preference?"

She immediately tells me a specific brand and model. I search it up and add to cart. I need to set up something with these families too. I am not going to be able to visit them all any time soon. I pull up the file I created with the names and numbers that Devon gave me. Ok, Brooks family. Let's see, spirit affinity and they live in Canada.

Phone number… I tap the number into my phone and hit send.

The phone rings a while before a man's voice answers, "Hello."

"Hello, my name is Fate. I am looking for the Brooks family. Do I have the correct number?"

"This is Herman Brooks. How can I help you?"

"Well," Shit.. I did not think this through. "Have you… Does your family remember the Chronicler?"

"Yeah, but she hasn't been around in a century or so. We have spoken to the guy a few times."

"As it turns out, the Chronicler is back. Because she is me. I am her. I'm the Chronicler."

I hear him sigh on the other end of the line, "And what will you be wanting from us? Assuming you are in fact, the Chronicler."

"I understand why you would be skeptical, I would be in your place. But, I am who I say I am. Have you had many people call you up saying they were me?"

"Um, no. No one has."

"So no one has ever tried to pretend to be me in a century or so and you are concerned that someone will now? Really?"

"When you put it that way I guess it doesn't make as much sense as it seemed to when I had the thought."

"I do understand inherent suspicion. I don't trust people out of the gate either. But, I think maybe considering the facts you can at least hear me out."

"That seems reasonable, what can we do for you Mrs?"

"Oh, let's keep this informal. Fate works just fine. Ok, so, while I had initially planned to seek out each of the thirteen families, after meeting the Hale family—"

"Oh no, you started with them?"

"You've met them?"

"Not personally but my grandmother has told stories about them. What must you think of all of us?"

"I try not to judge a group based on the actions of one. As I was saying, after meeting them and with the foundation work I am currently doing, I realize that I won't have time to traipse the world seeking each of you. So, I would like for you to come see me. I will be calling each of the remaining twelve, well, eleven after your family, to descend upon North Carolina with the books they have collected. I wouldn't ask that you stay long, if you didn't want to. Only that you come and we can meet each other. You can pass on the books you have and I can set the contract to not siphon off your magic further."

"I think perhaps we can do that. Say, where were you all this time?"

"I was dead for a large part of it."

"Oh my. And what are you now?"

"Very much alive. I was reincarnated many times. But this job finds me anyway, ha. No really, I did reincarnate. I should be here for a very long time now." If no one manages to figure out a way to kill me…

"Erm, very well. Can I reach you back at this number? I need to talk to the rest of the family to get this scheduled, and it may take a minute."

"You can. You can also text me at this number, if you like."

"Oh yes, that is much easier. Thank you! I'll be in touch shortly."

"Thank you! I look forward to hearing from you!" I hit the end button and look up to find Memré watching in amazement. "What?"

"He was so polite the whole time. He honestly suspected you might be a lunatic but was unfailingly polite. Where are they from?"

I shrug, "Canada."

"Well no fucking wonder. Most of them are so nice that all the sweet makes me a little ill. They're coming here?"

"Eventually. May take more convincing. He needs to talk to the family."

My phone rings and it's Maggie, I wonder if one of the properties has a problem? "Hi Maggie! How are you?"

"I am great, and thankfully my life isn't nearly so exciting as yours. But there is a wolf in my office looking for you."

"A wolf in your office? An actual wolf or like a shifter wolf? I really hope actual wolves aren't searching for me."

"Nope, shifter. Distantly related to my husband. But, he says you left an earring in his ambulance? Fate, what the hell would you need an ambulance for?"

"OH! Oh! I think I know who that is! And I didn't need an ambulance. The cops showed up when Griselda," my throat closes up and I have to swallow the huge lump there to go on, "when that happened. The bullet passed through my shoulder so they insisted I be looked at. But I don't think that I was wearing earrings that day."

"Really? How sneaky of him, he has an earring here with him. He showed it to me, that and him being an EMT is why I called."

Laughing I tell her, "You know, he went to so much trouble to find me. Give him my address and tell him to come by in a couple days. It will give me time to tell the guys before he shows up."

Maggie laughs and we end the call. Memré asks as soon as I set the phone down, "You have another one?"

Shrugging I reply, "Maybe? He felt kind of like Charles did at first except with less creepy to him. A lot less of the creepy."

"Holy shit. What do you think the guys are going to say?"

"Mmmm, I don't think they will be thrilled. I guess I need to go break the news to them. I'll just finish this order so the house can be furnished," I click the pay now button and enter all the information. That done I close the laptop and stand, "Ok, off to face my doom…"

"Well, you'll never be bored. A different sausage any time you get tired of one. They seem well behaved too. Could your mom maybe hook me up?"

I laugh all the way down the hall after I tell her, "I'll ask," and she immediately hollers back that she was just joking and I better fucking not.

Four

I FIND them in the billiards room, such a fancy name for a room with a pool table. I walk in and Devon steps over to greet me while Charles makes his shot. Devon wraps his arms around me and spins me so my back is to the pool table before he runs his hands down my back to cup my ass firmly. He presses his lips to mine and the kiss stokes the fire between us, quickly deepening and causing my flames to dance across my body until I hear something hit the wall. Devon lets me down with a grin and I look around to see Charles shaking his head. Realizing what Devon did I turn back to him and shake a finger at him, he just laughs.

Charles says, "It would make him much more contrite if you came over to comfort me." Grinning I walk over to him and wrap my arms around his neck, standing on tip toes to kiss him. I hear his cue hit the floor with a clatter as his arms wrap around me and lift me off my feet. My flames dance across me once again as Charles turns the kiss into a whole mood. I break the kiss and tell him to put me down, I did actually seek them out for a reason. Devon sets the ball on the table as I step back from Charles, who leans down to pick up his cue.

I lean on the edge of the pool table and the guys wait for me to speak. Damn this is hard. "So," I watch as they both cross their arms over their chests, "remember the EMS guy?"

Charles raises a brow and Devon says, "What about him?"

"Well, he tracked Maggie down to return an earring that he says I left in the ambulance."

Charles growls, "You weren't wearing any earrings."

"I know. But you remember how things got a little flirty? He kind of feels like you did in the beginning Charles, just less creepy than you were."

"Great. New guy and I'm creepy."

Devon chuckles, "You were. Still are in my book. But the ambulance guy, You think he's like one of us? A possible bond?"

"I do. I don't know how. But he went to some lengths to find a way to get in contact with me. I don't think he had any choice."

They look at each other, back at me and in unison say, "I want to talk to your mom."

"Well, I need to train anyway. And I have some other things to see about while I'm down there." I swap out my work clothing for the exercise gear I wear to train with the snap of my fingers. "Would you like to have the quick clothing change or did you want to go do it yourself?"

Charles smirks, "I never want to do it myself unless its you."

Devon elbows him as he says, "Yes please."

I snap my fingers and they are in the matching suits, that leave nothing to the imagination. Goddess I love those suits! Focus. I stand and take their hands, moments later I open my eyes to the Underworld. Cerberus runs over from the door, barking and communicating, *You're here! It has been soooo long! Why were you gone so long? Did you bring them to play? Will we play today?*

Laughing I say, "Yes, I brought them to play. But we need to see mom and dad first. Lead the way?"

Cerberus is very excited to play today and immediately agrees to take us to my parents. He asks after his children and I tell them that they have taken to sleeping on the bed with us at night but the guys have no idea. He laughs and nudges open the door to my parents' office. They stand as we enter, both rounding their desks to come hug me hello. I think I will never tire of their hugs. They are everything I could have hoped to have in parents. I never knew I could enjoy having parents so much. It seemed so far out of reach before. They release me and Hades greets the guys, "Hello Cretins. Cerberus is very excited to have you over to play."

Fate

Devon groans, "I'm sure he is. But first, I, uh, we have a question for you Persephone."

Mom looks over to the guys, "Yes?"

Devon pulls at the neckline of his suit, "This guy showed up and—"

Charles interrupts, "Are there more like us? More possible bonds for Fate?"

My mother smiles so sweetly as she tells them, "Yes, there are."

"How many?" Devon asks as my father starts laughing.

Persephone shrugs one shoulder, "I lost count. I started adding people after Charles started killing her and you continually failed to prevent it."

Hades laughter grows louder and he falls down he is laughing so hard. Cerberus decides to throw himself on his back and laugh too, though he isn't quite sure why more mates for me is so upsetting for the guys.

She continues as my father calms himself, "Fate will know when they can't resist seeking her out. If she doesn't care for the person all she has to do is reject the bond. They will be released as will she."

Charles' eyes narrow, "I notice you said they, so you did this to souls didn't you?"

"I did." I turn to help my father up because now I want to laugh. He is still grinning and watching the guys faces as I help him upright.

Devon's eyes go round, "So the next one could be anyone? We can't even leave her alone in a baby shower without the worry that she could come home with a new mate? Fuuuck. The house is going to be overrun with all of us."

Hades chuckles, "She doesn't have to accept them all you know. It is very much up to her and them whether they want to continue the bond."

Devon throws his hands up, "Yes, but with them coming out of the woodwork who knows how many there will be! This has been going on for over a hundred years, I am guessing," he looks over at my mother who shrugs and studies her nails, "and that is a lot of time to be picking up stray souls for your daughter. There could be hundreds!"

Giggling I tell him, "I don't think I could deal with hundreds. I mean, where would I find a bed that big?" My father starts laughing all over again and my mother joins in while Devon glares at me. Charles walks over and pulls me into his arms, "You have as many as you want love, I just want you happy."

Devon mutters, "Kiss-ass."

My father laughs, "He may be a kiss-ass but I would like to point out that he was successful in his aims for a long time. Perhaps you should try a little ass-kissing? It might help."

My mother laughs loudly at that and her laughter is contagious, it gets us all going. Once everyone has calmed and composed themselves I screw up the courage to ask my questions. "Now that the guys have asked their questions, I have my own." It is so weird how my parents just give me their attention like what I have to say is important to them. Weird as it is, I really like it. "I need some answers about the past that no one living can provide. I—is it possible to talk to some of the souls?"

My mother frowns, "It is possible, assuming they are not recycled already. Who?"

I swallow, "My adoptive parents and Griselda."

"Oh! Yes! Certainly."

"And could you tell me some about the other gods? I feel like I should know things that are less mythology and more truth. For instance, you," I point to my mother, "are a kidnapping victim that ended up with a little stockholm syndrome. Mostly the world ignores that you are queen of the Underworld and they definitely do not believe you chose this. So I figure the other stories are equally rewritten."

Both my parents roll their eyes, and my mother says, "They are. Yes. We can tell you about the other gods, it will be good to add that to your education. For now, Cerberus, take the boys to training. Your father will join them soon, but he is better at finding specific souls than I am."

Five

I keep on working in the dining room once Fate goes off to handle her men. Holy hell, two already and a third waiting in the wings. What is she going to do with them all? It's been so long since I had sex I don't know if I can remember how to, if I were to find someone I was willing to let be that close to me. After I put my ex in prison, I just haven't wanted anyone since.

Of course, the one guy that has stirred things up down there for the first time in years just has to be a ridiculously overbearing, insufferable vampire. And oh look, here he is. I duck my head and focus on my screen but he takes the chair next to me anyway.

I straighten and narrow my eyes at him, "Can I help you?"

He smiles wide, "Yes. You could have dinner with me."

"I—Wha—Why would you want to have dinner with me when I have made it so very clear that I don't want to spend time with you?"

His smile grows as he leans toward me, "Because I can smell the lie. When I walk in the room I can hear your heart beat faster. I smell the pheromones released from your yearning body. Has anyone ever told you that you smell of citrus and vanilla? Your scent fills the room you are in, no matter who else is in the room with you till all I can smell is you."

"You can smell all that?"

He taps the side of his nose, "A vampire's nose is very sensitive. I can smell a great many things that the average human can't. For instance, I can smell that you want me right now, though you swear you want nothing to do with me. I smell fear too and I am curious about that. Why would wanting me make you fearful? Are you concerned I would bite you?"

I look away. Damned vampires. "I am not afraid you would bite me without permission, Fate would do very bad things to you. I am concerned you would fool me into believing you are a decent person and I very much don't want to be fooled like that again." I feel tears burning at the back of my eyes and I close my computer, standing and heading for the shelter of my suite. Looking at the floor as I walk I don't see him move and I run into him standing in the door way. He is a solid wall and I barreled into him, he catches my arms before I can fall backward. The touch of his hands sets all my nerve endings on fire.

"I am so sorry, I did not mean to hurt you. I only want to get to know you better." He releases an arm and puts a finger to my chin, gently pressing me to look at his face, "I don't know who they are or what they did but I can promise I won't lie or hide what I am. I am a vampire. I have less problems with killing than humans generally appreciate, no matter how choosy I am with my prey. I am an elder, I rule with an iron fist in most cases, I will not tolerate disobedience that puts us all in danger. I guard those I consider mine. And I would very much like to get to know you, if you can see your way clear to give me a chance."

I do a fine imitation of a fish out of water, my mouth opening and closing with no sound emerging. I manage to swallow and gather my wits, "I need to think about it. What if you change?"

"Of course I will change, that is the way of things."

"What if you change in a way that I can't accept?"

"Then we part ways. You get used to that sort of thing when you live as long as I have. Sometimes things end. I can say no one has ever left me in disgust if that is your concern."

I look away and he drops his hands though he doesn't move away from me. I tell him, "One dinner. That's all. One dinner and if that goes well, maybe I'll think about another."

He grins as I look up at him, "Good. That is all I ask, is for the opportunity to get to know you. Tomorrow evening good for you?"

"So soon?"

"Heh, yes. I need to make some preparations."

I narrow my eyes at him, "Don't forget I can drop you in a hole or crush you with a rock if you act the fool."

He laughs as he turns and heads down the hall, "I wouldn't dream of it."

Six

NATASHA

THE SHOWER HELPED LESS than I hoped but I am up and moving now. Walking back out I can feel Billy's appreciative gaze but I ignore it. I just want to start with sorting these things. Dipping into the closet I throw on some leggings and a t-shirt. Not my usual style but today isn't my usual day. Fate told me that I could take over the library in this place and spell it as I need to, I think that is the best idea. Not that there are many that could break in with out facing a lot of consequences. Like Trust and Kindness. Weirdest names ever for hellhounds. I expected Spike or Fang or Killer.

Coming out of the closet I look over at Billy, "I need to get all these books to the library downstairs. Fate said I could take it over for these, so that is what I am going to do. Maybe we can get the bodyguards to help? Do you think they would?"

Billy rises from the bed and walks over to take my hands, "I know they would. I will get them now."

I pull him close and hug him before he can leave, "Thank you."

He kisses the top of my head and holds me tight. "Always here for you, however you need me."

He is gone with a whisper of air and I look around at the stacks. I start sorting them into predominant elements. By the time they get back I have multiple stacks of each going. I quickly explain the sorting and they tell me they will keep them sorted this way downstairs too. It seems like no time passes but the books are all downstairs and I am left looking at a room still half full with my Gram's magical trinkets.

I pick up a cameo from a nearby pile, it is old and lovely. But when worn by a woman with a broken heart it creates a siren-like effect. Men are drawn to her like like bears to poisoned honey, her very skin will be poisonous to them as long as she wears the cameo. A person content can wear it with no ill effects, for them it is a regular piece of jewelry.

I set the cameo down. My Grams knew every one of these pieces. She collected them from owners that were afraid of them, or concerned that they would be misused after they passed, and some that she found being sold as haunted. I let my eyes wander and take it all in, I feel a little closer to my Grams with all this in here. Silly. She isn't here with these things and I have work to do. A deep breath and I leave the room to find the library in this place.

I find Billy sitting in the library waiting for me, my heart swells with love for him. I haven't known him that long but he feels like forever in my arms. His care and concern for me are amazing. Right now, I don't know how I would function without him. Well, I do. Because I know Fate and Memré would be here if they didn't think he was taking care of me well enough. I walk over to him and he leans forward in the chair, reaching out to pull me down into his lap.

I rest my head on his shoulder as I look around the library. Shelves line the walls and they are mostly empty. All of us had some books, but not enough between us to fill a quarter of this space. I wonder what it looked like when Penelope lived here? Did she have an amazing collection that was the envy of all who visited?

Billy rubs my arm, "Is this too much for today? You don't have to finish this today. The beauty of being a vampire is that you have time. All the time in the world."

I snuggle into him, "No, I am good. As good as I can be. I was wondering what this library looked like when Penelope lived here. But now, I think I am ready to start shelving books."

I stand and he stands too. I go to the first pile, fire. Looking around I ask Billy, "How should I do this? Use the rows horizontally with books in each element marching across the room or vertically with each element stretching to the ceiling?"

A voice comes from behind us, "Vertical in order of age. The oldest books at the top and the newest to the bottom." We spin around in surprise to find Penelope hovering across the room, still transparent but visible.

"Jaysus Penelope! Make a noise when you come in or something!"

It looks like she blushes a little, which is weird. "My apologies, I haven't interacted with people politely in a very long time."

"It's fine, just startled us as we thought there was no one else in here. Vertical in order of age? I like it. What, if you don't mind me asking, did this library look like when you…erm, were in control of it?"

She lifts a side of her mouth in a little half smile, "It was filled with books. I had reading spaces throughout the room, little nooks for one to sit and read away an afternoon. I kept the oldest books, the hardest to replace, on the top shelves because adults are sometimes worse than children. I watch as she floats through the room, looking at the shelves and reminiscing. She disappears toward the other end of the room. I look at Billy, "You heard the lady, vertical in order of age. Let's get this pile sorted by apparent age and then we'll work at putting them on the shelves."

Seven

FATE

I WAIT ANXIOUSLY with my mom while dad collects two of the souls I want to talk to. She holds my hand and pats it occasionally while telling me, "You can do this. They won't be the same as when you knew them. Whatever hangups they had will be gone, the emotions attached to the things that happened or that they did just won't be there for them. While they have full recall of their lives past, it is like a really vivid dream they had last week."

I nod and take a deep breath. In just a few minutes I am going to see the people that raised me for the first time since they died. The people that treated me like garbage for most of that time, for all that I had everything I needed physically. "Do you think they will feel remorse?"

My mother looks away, "They might. Some do and others not so much." She looks back at me, "They may feel justified in their actions and think you are in the wrong for being upset. Or for not going along with their plan for you. It is difficult to tell."

I am staring off into the distance when my father walks through the wall in front of me, my adopted parents walking along behind him. They don't look very happy and my stomach flips, I suddenly have a very real fear that they are going to prove themselves to be the not remorseful kind. I don't know how much information I am going to get out of them. My adopted mother Diane spots me and grabs my adopted father Kevin's arm, pointing at me and looking angry. My mom squeezes my hand lightly, "Remember, they are here at your bidding and have no power over you. If you tire of them we can send them back."

I nod and stand as they draw near. Diane looks me up and down, "I see you got the glamour removed."

"I did. I don't need glasses anymore."

Kevin crosses his arms, "Glasses seem a small price to pay to fit in."

My heart shatters into a million pieces. My hand absently rubbing at my chest over where my heart should be I tell them, "I didn't call you here to talk about the glamour. Well, not about that specifically. Was there a reason why you set your daughter to invading my mind?"

Kevin has the nerve to look smug, "Our Demeter came to us and told us that it would be necessary to monitor you closely, to keep you from becoming a dark one like your birth parents."

Diane picks up where he leaves off, "She said the seed of evil was born in you and we must do all in our power to root it out. That was why she sent us looking for you, looking for the child that would be mysteriously abandoned in a remote place. She said you would bring about a great evil if we did not stop you. It looks like we failed."

My mouth is hanging open, I can't believe what she just said. "You were working for her the whole time? You only adopted me at her direction? You were that horrible to your own child just for Demeter?"

Diane sneers at me, "Pru was never our child! You put her there! I wasn't supposed to be able to have children. Then you had to interfere and suddenly I am pregnant and Demeter is insisting that I keep the child because she will be useful to monitor you, and I never wanted you either! I didn't want to be a parent! You should never have—"

My father snaps his fingers and Diane disappears mid-rant. Kevin looks frightened as my father turns his gaze to him. The flames dancing on Hades skin reflect in Kevin's eyes, "You. Answer any questions she has and keep a civil tongue in your mouth or I will remove it and you will spend eternity dripping blood from the open wound where your tongue used to rest."

Kevin's eyes are saucers as he swallows and looks to me, "Wh- How, um, what would you like to know?"

"Did I understand what Diane said correctly? You were sent to find me by Demeter?"

"Yes. She sent all her devotees out to find the child she said would bring great evil to the world. We were lucky and found you. She made sure we never wanted for anything as a reward. It was still hard on Diane, she hated being a mother and then you gave her Pru."

"What do you mean I gave her Pru?"

"I mean, we never had sex with each other. I was gay, she was a lesbian. We were together for cover. The world was not good to people that weren't straight back then so we just gave them the appearance they wanted and no one ever looked any deeper. We were very good friends but we never had sex. There was no way for her to get pregnant. Then you laid your hand on her belly and said sister. She was horrified. Even more so when she turned up pregnant and Demeter told her to keep the child."

"Oh no. I'm so sorry. That's terrible."

Kevin waves a hand in my direction as if to wipe it all away, "You know, it was a long time ago. I wasn't angry like Diane, but it wasn't my body. I just thought it was a kid with too much power and we had no thought to get you trained. If anything we planned that you wouldn't be trained because that would keep you easier to control. You seemed to know that she was really upset at you after that. You tried to get close to her, it looked like you wanted to fix the problem but she already had orders to keep it. Demeter had planned to come get you much sooner, but events conspired against her." He tugs at the collar of his shirt as he glances toward Hades, "Is there anything else you wanted to know?"

"Did she say what," I look down at the smooth rock

floor, I can't watch him answer this, "she wanted me for? What she planned for me once she collected me?"

I keep my eyes on the floor as Kevin says, "She said that she needed your body. She would be removing your soul and consigning it to a prison where you would never be able to hurt anyone again and your body would be given to another."

I feel the tears pricking my eyelids as I keep my gaze on a floor I can no longer see, "And you were both all right with that?"

"Yes? We didn't think we would be keeping you for very long and we were certain that Demeter would do what was best for all. She is the harvest mother after all."

"I-I don't have any more questions for him. Thank you for your honesty."

My mother draws me into her embrace as the sobs begin. She murmurs things as I cry, they sound soothing though I can't hear what she is saying. The pieces of my broken heart are washed by my tears and eventually they don't feel quite so jagged. I wipe my eyes as Persephone releases me. She takes my face in her hands, "Child, those people are blinded by Demeter. You were always desperately wanted by us. We only sent you away because I thought to protect you. I didn't realize that she had figured out what I was doing. I am so sorry they found you."

Sniffling I look up at her, "It's okay Mom. It just hurts is all. I cared for them even if they didn't care for me. Some little part always hoped that maybe they did care, way down inside."

Hades steps up behind her, "That is natural sweetheart. As is the pain you feel. Just know we love you and we are here for you."

Hades hands me a handkerchief and I notice the flames are still crawling across his skin, spiky and angry looking. Looking at his face I ask, "Are you all right?"

He looks surprised at the question and quickly looks at his own hand. With a frown he says, "Damned flames. Yes. I am fine, just angry on your behalf is all. And jealous. These people got to spend the time with you that we desperately wanted to spend with you and they were terrible. They only sought you out because of Demeter's meddling, which was the only reason you were away from us to begin with. I would really like to end this once and for all but I have to be a responsible god and not a stinking egotistical asshat of a goddess with less brains than a bar stool."

I chuckle, "Less brains than a bar stool? Is that possible?"

Mom raises a brow, "Zeus once turned himself into a bar stool so that a woman he had been after would sit on his face. She was not best pleased and she grabbed an axe off the wall. She was a powerful witch, I think I heard that she cursed him after that but I could be wrong."

"Oh no. That is horrid. Why— Never mind. I don't want or need to know." Blowing my nose I disappear the handkerchief to the laundry at the house. Looking to my father, "I think I am ready to talk to Griselda now. And can we get a visit going for her and Natasha? I think, I know it would really help her out while she is dealing with her mother."

My dad nods, "It can be done, because she is your friend and because she is a protector. Shame about her mother being unfit, Griselda was saddened to have to register her that way."

"When did she do that?"

My parents look at each other and Mom says, "Nearly fifty years ago? Give or take a few."

"She knew that long ago? I really have so many questions for her."

Hades blinks out and quickly returns with a much younger looking Griselda. I stand when she walks in and she runs the last few steps over to envelope me in a hug. Releasing me she keeps hold of my shoulders and looks me over, "You look sad but mostly happier. Charles and Devon are getting along for you? How's my Natasha? And what made you cry?"

My mother laughs as I say, "Yes, they are getting along for me. They are here now but off training. Natasha, she misses you and she is having a hard time dealing with her mom. I am going to bring her to visit you very soon. As for the crying, well, I needed some answers from Diane and Kevin."

"Oh! They still can't be decent. Assholes." She looks to Hades and Persephone, "You might think about cooking those two a bit, they may not feel any guilt for things they did but they were no less awful for their lack. They managed to be at least equal to my own daughter in that respect."

My parents nod and step away to converse. I would not want to be in Kevin and Diane's shoes right now. "Griselda, what do you mean equal to your daughter? How bad is she? I mean, you and Natasha are amazing."

She grimaces and sits down. I sit too as she starts to speak, "She is bad. A lot more bad than I ever wanted to admit while I lived, as much as that shames me now. She did terrible things as a child, I had to ward her room and bind her to keep her from using her powers to harm. By the time she was in high school she seemed to be in control. But then the whispers started. I had released her from the binding years before that, she seemed to have changed. I wanted to believe she had changed. Maybe I saw things that weren't true because I needed to believe she wasn't the terrible person I suspected she could be." She shrugs and continues, "People would come to me, whispering about bad things happening to anyone that crossed her. Anyone that crossed Myra would suddenly fall ill or sprain an ankle. I caught her trying to take trinkets from the house on numerous occasions and I created a spell keyed to her so that any time she touched one of them they started screaming and emitting flashes of light that would be seen only by her and would be absolutely blinding. She hated me for it. I told myself it was just growing pains. Then she married Sami and I thought she would settle down. She had Natasha and I thought I could breathe again, then I saw the scratches on my sweet Natasha. I had her for the night and I was giving her a bath, she had terrible scratches on her back. She was barely a year. I did a seeing right then to find out how and it broke my heart. I kept her for weeks after that and only relented after I wrapped her in spells so thick I knew Myra would never get through them." Griselda looks me in the eye, "She was trying to take power from her baby. My baby wanted to steal the power from her own baby. I cursed her womb that she would never have another child. I couldn't risk it that she would move away and have one that I didn't know about and she would be free to do as she pleased with."

"Oh Grams. I am so sorry. That does explain some things that happened at the funeral."

She looks sharply at me, "What happened? Tell me she didn't get any of the trinkets!"

"No, she didn't. We went to your house and though people had tried to get in they were unsuccessful. We kept it sealed off from everyone else while we worked to collect all the books and all the trinkets. I transported them to our house, which was already heavily warded. Myra had already mentioned your jewelry box and when we realized the things held in it were some of the worst we transported that still closed. But not before I created a replica. Exactly the same feel, look, and items within but none of the power, no matter that it felt like they were powerful. When it seemed everyone was busy Myra grabbed the jewelry box and took it to her car, though Natasha had already expressly told her she could not have it. The messages after that weren't nice."

"Oh my poor girl. Is she okay? Is Billy with her?"

"She is as good as she can be. She misses you. Billy is taking very good care of her and we are there. I plan to bring her to visit you very soon. I think that will help her more than anything. She didn't know, well, I mean, I know you told her some things but she didn't grasp how awful her mom would be. It hurts."

Griselda shakes her head, "I am not surprised. It is hard to be prepared for that even when you were warned. No one wants to believe a daughter or a mother could be so terrible. You are going to bring her soon, yes?"

"I am. Now, is there anything about my adopted parents that I need to know? Things that maybe they haven't told me? Things I wouldn't know to ask?"

"Hmm, let's see. Your dad told me some as we walked here. So they told you it wasn't a real marriage, just one of convenience and safety for the two of them. Not that it matters beyond that Diane never wanted children. She was one of Myra's friends in school, one that was always her bestie. They made it appear that they went their separate ways after high school, but they continued the friendship quietly. That may be something to look into. Diane and Kevin never trusted me much so I don't know a whole lot beyond that. I think I know what trinket Myra was after. She has been trying to get this amulet created by a powerful witch for a very long time."

"What does the amulet do? Why does she want it?"

"The amulet allows for control of one person's body by another person."

"Oh. Oh my. Is there any species it won't work on?"

"Probably not the gods… But vampires, shifters, witches; no one else would be immune to it. If they think you are still just a witch or vampire…"

"They will want to use it to control me. So to some extent she is likely involved in this mess with Demeter."

Eight

AFTER TALKING with Griselda I spend some time with my parents before I take my guys home. Natasha, Memré, and I curl up on a couch, talking about the amulet and her mom with fancy margaritas. She is sad about her mom but my friend is so strong, she said that she always saw something off in her mom but she didn't know what it was and nothing ever happened. She thought it was her imagination until now. It really perked her up knowing that she would get to visit her Grams soon.

This afternoon though, has my heart rate up and the guys somewhat annoyed. Well, maybe annoyed is the wrong word. I think they both feel a little insecure knowing I am meeting with Julian today and that I am excited about it. Although I like the way Charles handles his insecurities, it does make me grateful for my lack of neighbors to see my light show.

Devon on the other hand has preferred to be more

loving to deal with his issues and I can't seem to be mad about that either. Both of these methods have meant that my time to work today has been mostly shot. Benny is door man today and he just let me know that Julian has arrived. He put him in the closest sitting room to the kitchen. I feel like that was possibly planned by Devon and Charles but I don't mind if they are a little protective.

As I open the door and walk into the sitting room Julian turns away from a window with a smile, "Hello gorgeous."

I smile at him and close the door behind me. Gesturing to the chairs, "Have a seat please." I walk over and take my own seat as he sits, "You know Julian, I have wracked my brain but I cannot recall having worn earrings the day that I saw you."

"You didn't," he says with a cheeky grin. "That didn't stop me from buying a pair to convince Maggie to get in touch with you."

"Fair enough. I am curious though, why you didn't just look it all up on the paperwork from that day?"

"HIPPA. I am not trying to lose my license. I knew I had other ways to find you and I am pretty certain that I was meant to find you."

My eyes widen, "Why do you say that?"

"Because I have been dreaming of you all my life. I am a little confused by the more recent dreams, your appearance changed pretty drastically between one night and the next. Though, the fuzziness surrounding you went away too."

"Oh. You saw all that? Um, well, that is a long story. The short version is that there was a powerful glamour placed on me when I was very young. It is gone now."

He leans forward in his chair, "I would be very interested to hear the entire story. Perhaps over dinner?"

"I think we need to discuss some things before we go there. The first being that my mother is Persephone and she picked up a habit of assigning me mates every time she found a likely soul. But, you don't have to accept that, she left us an out. I can release you from the bond and you can walk away to a life without dreams of me."

Julian leaves his seat to kneel in front of me and take my hands, "That sounds like a terrible idea. I like those dreams and the idea of getting to live them makes me very happy. I don't want to be released."

"Then you need to know that Devon and Charles are also my mates, you would be one of three so far. My mom may have gotten a little carried away with this whole mates for her daughter thing."

"I know about them. At least, I know they exist. My dreams showed me that. So I came prepared to accept that. Once I saw you in person I knew the dreams were all true. It took me a minute to get right with that part, but after I accepted those dreams as true, the rest was a cake walk."

He has been leaning in, closer and closer as he spoke. It feels like there is a magnet between us as I lean froward the last inch so our lips touch. The kiss is like an explosion, want and need setting me aflame as I am pressed against him, our bodies flush as I slide out of the chair to my knees. He breaks the kiss and draws back a little, "So the flames are real? This is wild." He runs his hands up my back and down my arms, watching the flames dance as he does. "What do I need to do to convince you to keep me?"

I smile, "I am convinced, now you need to convince Devon and Charles." We stand and he looks to the door, "They will not be as easily convinced as I am. But their approval is important to me. Without it I will have to tell you good-bye."

He says, "That's fair." As the door opens to reveal Devon and Charles. "Ah, glad you are here. It would seem I need your approval."

Charles smirks and Devon's brows drop into a scowl. Devon growls, "Might be easier to talk about that if you weren't holding our woman."

I love being the independent woman I am but that growl of ownership sent shivers through my body and straight to my core. All three of them scent the air, inhaling deeply. Charles looks at Devon, "Say it again."

He scrunches his face at Charles, "Not while he is holding her dumbass."

Charles shrugs, "Fate," and he holds out a hand to me as he growls, "please come here my darling."

What is it with the growls and my whole body responding? My core clenched with the growled darling and I lean up to kiss Julian on the cheek, he turns his head quickly to kiss me lightly on the lips before he releases me to go to Charles. I cross the room to him and he envelopes me in his embrace as I wind my arms around his neck.

Lifting me off my feet he presses his face into the crook of my neck and I sigh with the pleasure of it. All too soon he sets me down, "We'll finish that soon, very soon. For now, it is our turn to interview him and make our decision. Go for a walk or something." He smacks my ass and gently pushes me out the door which he closes behind me.

Nine

PRU

I feel a strange presence drawing near. The closer it gets the happier Demeter gets. She sets me to preparing a platter of meats, cheeses, and fruit. She was much nicer before I came back without Fate's body. Since then she has been angry and mean. The house seems a lot smaller with her angry. I am just trying to make it through till I can get out of here. I think I still want Fate dead, but this with Demeter is not what I expected. I just worry, what happens if I leave and she finds me again? Will I ever be safe if I run away from here? And why am I not so angry at Fate anymore? She consumed my thoughts until after I got back and that makes me less than comfortable here. Because why would that disappear?

I see Demeter run to the front door and I hurry to get the platter finished and get out the champagne she had me chill. The glasses are out and I arrange it all on a large tray.

It would be difficult for me to carry this if I were still human. I wonder if she will let me go feed soon? I am getting hungry for blood and the raw meat isn't quite doing it for me. She brings in this presence I have felt drawing near and he is horrifying.

He looks like he is rotting, bits and pieces hanging loose. The mix of fur and flesh is strange and unholy, I have never seen anything like it. They ignore me as they walk into the living area. She seats him in the largest chair in the room telling him, "I had my girl prepare a tray for you. She should be in any moment."

I walk in behind her, careful to hide my revulsion. My face is neutral as I pour champagne for the two of them and place the platter on the table next to the creature's chair. I guess he must be some sort of royalty in her eyes, because she is definitely fawning over him like he is. I was going to sit in a chair but Demeter screamed in my head not to sit in the presence of my betters. I manage to keep myself from falling over and I walk to the kitchen, busying myself with cleaning up while I listen to them talking.

Demeter fills this beast in, "Her sister failed me when I sent her to collect Fate. They took the shot when she was surrounded by people and her assassin was immediately killed when the wrong person died. It is so hard to find good help!"

His voice is gravel as he tells her, "I know darling. You are the only one I have been able to trust all this time. But my body grows weak, the curse is eating away at me. The energy to keep it from consuming me is wearing me to the bone. I must have her, and soon."

"I know, my love, my Zeus." Holy crap, that creature in there is Zeus? What happened to him? And maybe I need to think about praying to a different god for aid in hiding. I tune back into the conversation as Demeter says, "I just don't know how we are going to separate her from all those idiots protecting her."

"I have an idea. I could go, tell her you are coming to get her. She must come away with me. If I feed on a human it will sustain me for long enough to get her back here to start the process. I can maintain my disguise that long and blink her back here. I can even get through her barrier by taking on the seeming of an animal, no one ever thinks to block out the animals."

Well that is terrifying. But maybe if they have Fate I can slip away…"Pru! Get in here!" I rush in there and Demeter tells me, "I need you to find a person. Someone no one will miss but young as possible. Ideally around nineteen to twenty five, older or younger than that has diminishing results. Bring them alive and do not feed from them! If you must, feed before you collect the human. He prefers women. Go! Return quickly!"

I leave the house with fear clawing at my bones. How am I going to do this?

Fate

Benny is walking to the sitting room and turns the corner just in time to see the door close behind me. He laughs and says, "Ah, Fate, there are some people at the gate that say you called them here? They gave the name Silseth."

"Hmm, let me… Oh! Yes! That is one of the families! Let them in and um, hmm. Bring them to the dining room where I usually work at, ok?"

"Sure thing." Benny takes off and I head for the dining room. I am pretty certain that Memré is working in her suite today. Avoiding a very persistent Malachi. I feel for her, but I see the fire in her every time they come near each other. I wonder how long before she can't stop herself with ghosts from her past?

I am drawn from my thoughts as Benny brings the Silseth family in. I walk over and hold my hand out to the woman in the lead, "Hello, my name is Fate. And you are?"

Her nose rises a bit in the air and she looks down it as she takes my hand, touching skin as little as possible, "I am Clarinda and these are Odonna, Raylan, and Uther. We are the Silseth family of Wyoming."

"What a pleasure it is to meet you. Please, sit and let us talk."

I take the space at the head of the table, leaving them to sort themselves on either side. They settle on the right side, all four of them. Looking down their long noses at me, as if I have wronged the world by existing. I feel annoyance rising but work to keep my face neutral as I ask, "Have you brought the books you collected?"

"We came to see if you were even the Chronicler. We have not seen the Chronicler in the flesh in many generations, how are we to believe you are her?"

Clarinda's voice makes me want to slap the snotty out of her. Instead I say, "Exactly how many people have come to you pretending to be me? I know the answer is zero. Have you not noticed the weakening of your powers? Throughout your family? I can end that or finish off the process, leaving your family powerless. I have not the time for this. Now," I stand, "you are called by your Chronicler. Will you honor your commitment or forfeit your power now?" My voice rose as I spoke, it was only when their eyes turned to saucers that I realized I was on fire again, blue flames crawling my body to match my agitation.

Clarinda looks to the others before looking back to me a sly glint in her eyes, "May we have a time to think about this?"

"No! That's it! Your powers are revoked! When you return with the books as your family agreed to do so many years ago, then I will think about reinstating them!"

Clarinda stands, rage plain on her face, I watch her try to call powers that no longer answer to her and a horrible realization dawn across her face. She screeches and launches herself at me, I throw a shield around the four of them. She hits the shield and falls back at her chair, caught before she falls farther by the one she introduced as Uther.

"Get out of my home. Do not return unless you are

ready to fulfill your family's promise and behave yourselves. The shield will not dissipate until you leave the
property, nor will it allow you to go anywhere but your car
and off the property. Be gone from my sight."

The family jumps into action, scurrying out of the
room past Ajah and Ryna, who appear to be holding back
giggles. They walk in and Ryna says, "We have been
listening from down the hall and came when we heard the
shriek. She does have a set of lungs on her. We arrived at
the door just in time to see her fall back on her companion.
Are you all good? You seem to be on fire."

I frown, "I know. I know. It happens when I get
emotional, it won't hurt anyone not trying to hurt me.
Mostly it just annoys me because it is a tell."

Ajah asks, "Can we put our hands in the flames? Just
to see?"

I hold out a flame covered arm for them to check out
the flames and they both run their hands through without
ever touching my skin, giggling all the while. Finished
experimenting with my flames they each put an arm
around the other, "Is there anything we can do for you?
Can we get you something? Want us to get the guys?"

"Ugh, no. They are busy talking with Julian, let's not
give them a reason to put that off. I think, I think I will just
wander the property a bit. Have a little walk. Trust and
Kindness are out there wandering somewhere, they will
come find me. You two go have fun. Gods you are both
adorable, you know that? I need to go sulk for a minute.
That family has me fired up."

The two of them burst into giggles again at that. I throw up my hands and let them fall to hit my hips. "I am going for a stroll on the property. Try to contain yourselves."

The give me a thumbs up as I walk past them. They are lucky they are so adorable, Ajah with her dark coloring and Ryna with her golden coloring, or it would be much easier to be annoyed with how cute they are.

Ten

FATE

The grounds are lovely though overgrown. I need to find someone to come take care of them. I stop to smell the roses on a much overgrown bush, it has a glorious scent. Walking on I see Trust and Kindness staying near but wandering about sniffing things and leaving me to my thoughts. Are they all going to be horrible? Obviously the Brook's family has told others, I can only hope that the Silseth family will let everyone else know that I am no longer willing to entertain nonsense.

Then there is Julian. His easy charm and sweet manner pull at me but I don't know what Charles and Devon will decide. I feel like I need to honor their wishes but I very much want to keep him. He feels like a piece of our puzzle. I think Charles will—

A man runs out of the woods, "Fate! I'm so glad I found you! Hurry!"

I throw shields up on myself and watch as Trust and Kindness flank the man in silence. "Who are you?"

He stops in front of me, "Zeus. Do you not recognize your grandfather?" I drop the shield because Zeus is actually my grandfather. "You need to come away with me right now. Demeter is on her way," he holds out a hand toward me, "come with me."

I step back, trepidation coursing through my body, Zeus doesn't help anyone. He has stayed neutral all this time, why help me now? Why come running out of the woods and not just appear in the house like my parents? I call for my parents, sending a mental cry for them.

Zeus cocks his head to one side, his eyes narrow, "You know I can hear that, right?" Trust and Kindness leap at him but he zaps them and they fall unmoving to the ground. He reaches out, grabs my arm and we disappear.

Ryna

A terrible screeching sounds through the house. Ajah and I look at each other and start running for the sound. We nearly crash into Hades and Persephone when they appeared in front of us. Skidding to a halt we missed them but immediately took off around them again. I can hear them behind us as we make it to the front sitting room where the noise seems to be coming from. There doesn't seem to be anything in the room as I stop in the middle of it. As I scan the room a second time the ghost appears, screaming, "He took her! He took her!"

Persephone walks over to speak with the ghost, for which I am profoundly grateful. I don't know what the hell to say to a screeching, or even a not screeching, ghost. At this point the room has filled and looking around there is only one person I do not see. Fate. I look at Ajah and her face is pinched, I know she has come to the same conclusion. I tune into what the ghost is telling Persephone, "—he looks shining and golden but he isn't what he seems. His soul is rotting and so is his body. He grabbed her and they disappeared. He killed the dogs. Persephone and Hades both look stricken and angry by this time. Hades flames are rolling off him and Persephone is glowing darkly. I didn't even know that was possible. Hades turns to Devon, Charles, and Julian, "You three come with me." They stride out of the room. Persephone is thanking the ghost, "Penelope, your help is so very appreciated. May I look at your recent memories so that I can see his face? See what you saw?"

The ghost nods and Persephone touches her head, it looks like she is solid for her. Her eyes fly open and she gasps, "No!"

<h1 style="text-align:center">Eleven</h1>

NATASHA

Hades returns to the room, carrying a dog over each shoulder. They have scorch marks on their fur but seem to be breathing. He lays them on a large cushion that appears in front of him, setting them down so very gently. Two bigger dogs appear next to the cushion and sit, looking very much like they are there to guard their friends.

Persephone waits patiently for him to finish before she tells Hades, "It was him. My father took her. He is part of this. He hurt Trust and Kindness. They were protecting our daughter. From him!" She is standing at this point and a wind I can't feel is whipping her clothing and hair. Her voice is rising with every word, "Zeus took our daughter to sacrifice her so that he may live! He is cursed and rotting from the inside and he. Took. Our. Daughter!"

The last word resounds through the house and probably the neighborhood. What she said is terrifying, how do we get her back from a god? I turn to Billy and grab him, hugging him close.

Persephone is not done as she lifts her arms to the sky, she calls out in a strange voice, "Hear my call! I will have what is mine, the battle begins now! Come to me, if you would be my ally! The Queen of the Underworld calls you to battle!"

The wind drops, Persephone's clothing falling into place. Hades mouth hangs open, "You are the most amazing creature and I am the luckiest god alive. When we get done, how about a vacation so that I may worship my goddess?"

Persephone nods to him, "Yes. But for now, they come." She looks to Devon and Charles, "You are how we will find her. Your mating bonds with her are activated and you will be able to zero in on her." She looks at Julian, "Unfortunately your bond is not yet activated so you will not be able to do this. Pay attention though. It may be useful if it is activated."

I clear my throat, "Excuse me. I don't mean to intrude, but how are we going to get Fate back? Did I hear you say battle? Isn't that going to expose everything? Do we have a plan of sorts? When you said Zeus, you didn't really mean high and mighty Zeus with the lightening and thunderbolts, right?"

Persephone's lips pick up on one side, "Yes, little guardian. Yes, it is that Zeus. You did hear me say battle. No one has challenged Zeus in all this time because of his allies. He has gone too far with the kidnapping of our daughter. There will be a battle, possibly more depending on how things go. It will begin here, but most humans will not be able to see it. The ones that do will think it a dream. Zeus will lose his throne. The gods will no longer have a petty ruler with less morals than a criminal. The plan is taking shape, but we need to wait for the others to arrive. Don't worry, it will take him, well, them quite some time before they can actually finish what they plan. She is a fully activated goddess, and they were not counting on that."

I bury my face in Billy's chest. I can't lose Fate too.

Twelve

Pru

It worked. It actually worked. The Beast caught Fate and now she is unconscious on the floor. I know I have wanted and tried to kill her for a long time but somehow I just feel pity for her lying there on the floor. Demeter yells at me to get her in the chair and tied up. Grabbing a chair I put it near her and hoist her up into it. Holding her in place I wrap the rope around her torso once and pull it tighter so she is upright. I wrap it around her a few more times before I use it to tie her hands together behind her. I didn't tie the knots as tightly as I could and I leave her hands wrapped loosely. I don't know if it will be enough to help her but it is all I can do.

I walk away from Fate and to the room I have been staying in since I got here. Sometimes when I hide they forget I am here. I sit against the wall next to the door and lean my head against it, focusing on hearing everything. I can hear Fate breathing quietly and her heart beating a steady pace, but she is still out.

The Beast is pissed that Fate has already become a fully activated goddess, whatever that means. He is giving Demeter hell about it.

"How could you let her become activated? You had one job all these years and you still managed to fuck it up every time!"

Demeter is actually sniveling, "I'm sorry! I did my best! They kept hiding her from me, I'm sorry! I sent everyone out after her, but I couldn't go myself! You set the sentence! If anyone caught me it would have been death for me! I did everything I could!"

I hear Zeus' heavy footsteps as he crosses the room and Demeter whimpers, "Then you didn't do everything. You should have been out there yourself. You could have found her if you really wanted to, I think you just want to keep me this way!"

"No! I swear it! I want my Zeus back! I want you hearty and hale like you were before! I miss all of you. I wish we could find the one that cursed you, none of this would be necessary. Oh love, it is always you. I love you. I just want you back. Don't you know I would do anything for you Zeus?"

Yuck. Hearing Demeter talk like that to that thing out there turns my stomach.

The Beast replies, "I do. I do. I'm just so frustrated. I

don't have another thousand years or so for another god to have a child. My time is running out. I don't want to leave you my darling. You have always understood me and my needs better than anyone else."

"Will you leave her? When you are well, will you leave her and never go back?"

"I will my darling. What use have I for a jealous shrew like Hera? She never understood my need for variety, for adventure. When I am well, I will be all yours my love."

"I think I know a way. To weaken her enough to be able to cast her soul from that body."

"How? What must we do?"

"We will need to drain her power. It will take at least three days before we can drain her enough to overpower her rejuvenation capabilities, but after three days of draining her we should be able to kill her, force her soul from the body and let you enter her body, claiming it for your own."

Enter? Does she mean? Ew, please tell me she does not mean what I think she means....

The Beast speaks again, "Oh love, that is perfect. Help me get started draining her. Her essence, her life force and her power will feed mine while we wait for her to be weak enough to kill."

My stomach roils with the implications of what he said. I know I wanted her dead, but not like this. Never like this. I don't even know for sure that I want her dead anymore. It seems like all the bitterness I had toward her has just dried up, leaving me empty and unsure. What do I do? I can't fight them. Even one of them is too strong for me. Scooting away from the doorway I lay down on my side and curl into a ball of fear and uncertainty.

Thirteen

My father's wife arrives first. Hera is a vision of loveliness and I know she hasn't always felt very charitable toward me. I can't really blame her for that either. We have come to be almost friends in the past hundred years or so. Meeting away from Olympus and my father. I welcome her warmly, "I am so glad you came. I must confess though, I have poor news to share."

Hera nods, "My husband has been gone from my sight for many weeks, and you are having troubles with Demeter, newly finished with her sentence."

I nod, "You are correct. Zeus is with Demeter and they have stolen my daughter. Zeus himself was the one come to collect her. The house ghost, Penelope, witnessed it all. She shared the memory with me and I can let you see it if you would. I must warn you, Zeus has been hiding things. More than his collusion with Demeter, he is… cursed.

Penelope was able to see through his illusion as it was meant for the living. Do you want to see this horror, knowing it will be exactly that?"

Hera closes her eyes for a moment. Opening them she looks me in the eye and extends her hands, palm up, "Show me." I place my hands gently on hers and she turns her hands, lining them up with mine so our palms are flush and her fingers intertwined with mine. She tells me, "So I will see it all, even if it hurts. I don't want you to stop showing me, whatever my reaction."

I nod. I would want no less and I won't dishonor her by trying to pull this punch. I open my mind to her, showing her the scene exactly as Penelope showed me. How Zeus came running out of the woods, Fate's uncertainty. The strange overlay of his usual visage atop the rotted, corpse-like creature he truly is. The injuring of Trust and Kindness. Zeus grabbing Fate and disappearing with her. I hear soft sobs from Hera as she watches but her hands grip mine tightly, not once does she waver in her determination to see it all.

The memory over I open my eyes to see Hera, tears streaming from her eyes and sorrow writ large across her face. "He can't come back from this. He can't be allowed. I know what is wrong with him, it is a curse. He had been chasing a woman and she wanted nothing to do with him. She denied him and denied him, then he changed himself into a bar stool. She sat on the stool unaware and he assaulted her. She jumped up and cursed him, the most fitting curse that came to mind. That woman was one of my priestesses. She was good and strong and would bow for no one she didn't deem worthy. She ran to my temple when she realized what she had done. It wasn't something she could take back, or that either of us would want her to take back. She cursed him that the outside appearance would match his spirit. All he had to do was become a better god and he could circumvent the curse." She releases my hands as she turns away, "When she died we thought the curse had just slid off him like water, because fifty years later there was still no evidence to be seen. I am glad this allowed her to pass with her conscience clear." She wipes her tears away with a sleeve and turns back to face me, "I am also so very sorry that one curse caused all of this. We thought it didn't work. That is no excuse for the mess we caused. I will stay and we will get your daughter back. Then, then I will go and make sure he has no where to hide. Have you had thoughts on who should rule the gods when all is said and done?"

My eyes widen and Hades steps up next to me, "I have not and I know her only thought has been to end all this. However, I think before we start this battle, we may need to make a decision. Leaving it up to a vote is likely to turn this into a war and cause strife within our ranks. If we present them with a decision as we begin, I think it will go better."

Hera nods, "I will think on it. I don't want it. I think I would like to go away from Olympus for a time. Maybe I will take a lover once I am a widow. You will put him in Tartarus, won't you?"

"I will. He can't be allowed in with the other souls."

Hera looks around and spies an empty chair off in the corner of this crowded room. "I need a few moments. Greet the others and I will think on who will be a better leader."

She walks slowly to the chair and sinks into it, her gaze out the window and her eyes heavy with sorrow. Hades wraps his arms around me, pressing his chest into my back and leaning his head on mine, "She will be okay. Hera is strong. No one that has been dealing with Zeus for this long could be otherwise. Let's give her some time while we welcome Poseidon. He has just arrived and is dripping in the hall."

We make our way through the crowd to find Poseidon in the hall, dripping exactly as my Hades said. "Poseidon, you couldn't even dry off?"

"Ah Persephone, gorgeous as ever. Have you tired of the Underworld yet? Want to come explore the wonders of the sea?"

I feel Hades looming over me, "Brother, we aren't here to fight each other. Let us stick to the matter at hand."

Poseidon laughs, "Yes brother, the enemy of my enemy is my friend. What has happened?" He sweeps a hand across himself and the water disappears from him and the floor beneath him.

"It is Zeus. His crimes are catching up with him and he has taken our daughter with plans to kill her so he may live. We plan to retrieve her before he can carry out his plan."

Poseidon's cheery face has darkened as Hades spoke, "He kidnapped a goddess and plans to kill her so that he can live?"

I tell him, "Yes. He did. He kidnapped his own granddaughter from her home and plans to murder her for his own gain. Will you stand with us?"

Hera steps forward then, "And will you support this new goddess, this young one not hidebound in shoddy morals as our new Queen?"

My jaw drops, "What do you— We don't even know if she would. That is so much for one so young!"

Hera inclines her head in agreement. "It is a lot for one so young. But she understands this new world in ways we do not. Her rule will be fair in ways that we won't understand at first. But, thanks to you she will have all the support she could possibly need with her mates and her friends. Most of the people here are already immortal, the few that aren't, she could grant it to if she chooses to do so. Your daughter could lead us into a better way to be. The people here adore her in a way that very few people love any of us."

Poseidon clears his throat, "Speaking as someone with a lot of things not pleasant to remember having done in their past, maybe that is what we need. Someone that inspires love instead of demanding it, right Aphrodite?"

Aphrodite steps away from the wall she was lounging against, "Oh my dear Poseidon, are you still mad about that? I haven't demanded anything in a very long time. It sounds like you all are talking about replacing Zeus. Who is it we are considering?"

"My daughter," I gesture to Hera, "She thinks we could do with a great many changes in how we do things and new leadership is the way to go. I don't disagree, but I am apprehensive about her taking all that on."

Aphrodite brushes against Poseidon causing him to shiver, "I think new leadership is a grand idea. While your daughter may be slightly favored toward you, she doesn't know any of us and we would all begin on an even playing ground. Hera, why? Why her?"

Hera sniffs at Aphrodite, they have never been super friendly with each other. "Because that entire crowd of people and one ghost in there adore her. I did some poking in their heads to find out why. She is just unilaterally good to them. One of her hired bodyguards had family issues and she just helped because she found out. Every one of her bodyguards is what most people would consider a low-life. One of the unwanted. She made them family. Her sense of justice is swift and certain, there was no hesitation in her when she killed the assassin. And get this, she didn't kill her assassin because they hurt her. She killed them because they killed an old woman. One of her mates is a man that spent years killing her. She managed to forgive him without even being aware that Demeter was the cause of his behavior. All he had to do was change."

"Shit. I didn't know people like that, gods like that, could exist." Aphrodite looks over at me, "I guess you did something right. I'll support her rule."

"As will I."

I turn to see Ares standing near, who knows how long he has been there, "Welcome Ares. I see you have been lurking long enough to get the full explanation. You support this as well?"

"I do. And I know that she will have you and Hades backing her up always, so she will have guidance and counsel from ones that have been here through the long years prior. You two know our tricks, even mine which is unfortunate but possibly a good thing. I have been known to get carried away occasionally."

Hekate steps out of the shadows, "I think occasionally is an understatement. I support the rule of Fate."

Athena walks out of a room, "As will I. We need a person more fit to rule, more fit to guide us than my father has ever been. The daughter of my sister is fit for the role."

Aphrodite chimes in to tell us, "I have good news. My beloved Hephaestus grew disgusted with Zeus many long years ago and quit making bolts for him. Zeus has none anymore, his favorite weapon is gone."

We hear a throat clear and turn to the doorway to find everyone in that room crowded in the entry. Charles elects himself speaker for the group, "Did we hear correctly that you all have just elected Fate to be queen over you all?"

My Hades answers him, "Yes cretin you did. Did you also hear the part about you having been under Demeter's control when you were killing Fate?"

"I did. I feel both relieved and angered, but mostly

angry. Will Fate be expected to go live on Mt. Olympus? If she is, are we going to be let in or no?"

I answer this time, "Yes, at least part time. And as for the rest, the ruler of Olympus makes the rules. What do you think Fate will do?"

He nods and responds, "She will eliminate that rule. She is everything you have described. Now, the important question, when do we go get her?"

Fourteen

FATE

I wake up bound to a chair. I feel weak in a way I never have before, I can't even create an air shield to bust out of these ropes. What is happening to me? Opening my eyes I look around as well as I can without moving my head.

"I know you are awake, you may as well lift your head and admire me."

My cover blown I do just that, looking around this smallish house I am in, tied to a chair. The ropes on my hands are a little loose, I may be able to do something with that. My gaze lands on my kidnapper, Zeus. I can see the almost translucent flow of energy from me to him. The bastard is siphoning off my energy! With the connection between us I can see that something is off about his appearance, though I don't know just what.

"How could I admire a man that kidnapped me? What

is your malfunction? Aren't you supposed to be my grand-father?" My head rocks back from a ringing slap and my eyes water even as I taste a little blood.

"Zeus is king of the gods and you will address him with respect you little trollop!"

"Let me guess, frumpy woman completely devoted to an utter asshole and in on shady dealings, you must be my grandmother, Demeter."

"And you are the bastard spawn of Hades and my daughter, now a means to an end."

"Bastard? I don't think that means what you think it means. You know my parents are married, right?"

Demeter throws her hands on her hips and leans down to look me in the eye, "They did so without my blessing and therefore they are not married."

"Hmm, controlling much?" Another ringing slap, this time to the other side. I am feeling more than a little sick of this bitch already.

Zeus crosses the room, "Demeter, my love. Let me handle this. Her allies will come soon, you must gather ours. Gather all you can, we must keep her until the ceremony can be completed."

Demeter simpers at Zeus, "Yes my love. I will gather warriors for you. You will be strong and virile once again. I will see to it if I have to kill the little bitch myself."

"My, my grandmother, so loving. What will the neighbors think?"

She ignores me and disappears. I have got to learn how to do that. Zeus turns his attention to me and is suddenly way more creepy. He walks across the room, squatting down and reaching up to run his hand along my cheek and down my chest between my breasts across my stomach and to a thigh, he squeezes it and runs his hand up and down it. "You are so beautiful Fate. A dark beauty just like your mother. It is such a shame that I have you in my control and cannot do what I would like."

"Get your hands off me. You make me sick. What kind of disgusting piece of garbage kidnaps his own grand-daughter?"

He runs his hand up my thigh to brush his thumb against the juncture of my thighs and I nearly vomit.

He steps back with a snort of disgust, "You should just be glad I don't show you my true visage. That is what would make you sick. What that bitch cursed me with, this rotting form."

I feel a slight relief that he is distracted into being angry and not touching me further. "Good. You probably deserve it if recent events are anything to go by!"

He leans into my face, spittle flying as he says, "You don't know what you're talking about! No one deserves this! No one! I spent years hiding my form so no one would guess that the king of the gods was a rotting shell." His visage morphs and he takes on this half man, half bull form. A little weird but whatever. Guess I know where all those stories originated. "You, little know-nothing, have no idea! But I just might show you! Oh yes, I just might. Let you see the disgusting mess that witch made of me. Would you like that? I don't think you will."

"Honestly, it probably just matches your shit personality." He has the head of a bull now and the eyes glow red as all the muscles pop and his fists clench. This might not be my best plan ever. But I won't make it easy for them, even if it hurts.

"Insolent child!" His voice rings through the house and probably the whole damn neighborhood. I bet there are kids out there cowering in place right now. "You would insult me even as I spare you this horror? Feast your gaze on my form now!"

I watch as his form morphs again, with most of the bulk dropping away. What is left is the stuff of nightmares. All the hair on his body is gone, one side of his face has rotted away, leaving yellowed bones and an eye floating in its socket, dry and blinded. The other side of his face shows the mottled black and yellow of rot, pus oozing from sores. His torso is a mass of sores and rotted flesh, some of it hanging in chunks or slivers. Parts of his legs are rotted to the bone, his pelvis is one giant cesspool, oozing sores and putrid flesh are all that was left resting in the cradle of the bones. As disgusting as that was, I still found it more palatable than him touching me no matter what he looked like.

I shrug as well as I can in the ropes, "Looks like my assessment was correct."

He loses his fucking mind over that and spends some time just stomping around bitching and yelling about the unfairness of it all. How very mediocre white guy of him.

Fifteen

After answering all of the questions the humans had we all move to the formal dining room. The gods lined up on one side of the table while the humans lined up on the other side.

There were considerably more humans than gods so I made the table and the room temporarily round. After the initial shock the humans nodded in approval, I imagine it made this seem more equal. Taking my seat I look to Charles and Devon as Hades slips an arm on the back of my chair, "You two are our link to her. If you reach down inside of you, you will be able to locate the general direction she is in if she is not nearby. The closer she is the easier it will be for you to pinpoint exactly where she is. If she were here in the house, you would be able to tell if she were in the training room looking out a particular window or upstairs in the bathroom off her bedroom. The farther away she is the more vague the direction will be. Give it a try."

Athena raises a brow at me and I shake my head at her. I know very well I could find her no matter where she is, even unto other dimensions. These men will be her protectors and they will help her keep the best of her human sentiments in ways that we did not. I watch the two men closely and Devon starts to smile but Charles' face screws up in confusion. "Problem Charles?"

He opens his eyes, "No. Not exactly, it isn't a problem, but I think I know where she is."

"That is what the idea of the exercise was…"

"Yes, but I mean I can get you an address because I think she is in the same place as the car that Pru stole. I have tracking on it, it has been parked at the same house for a while. I am pretty certain that is where she is at. I just need to pull up the tracker on my phone and I can give you an address." He pulls a phone out of his pocket and starts tapping away at it.

I look at Hades, "Do you think they will be watching for gods popping in?"

Aries laughs, "I fucking would. I would have an army of anything, human, creature, demigod, or god that I could convince to be on my side in this battle."

Athena nods, "I would as well. However, Zeus and Demeter have not been friendly with any god in a very long time, so I think that unless they win this battle, they will not have any gods on their side. Demigods, creatures, and humans are another thing. Demigods are easier to convince, at least the few that I know of still in existence. They have a penchant for killing each other and for being killed in general. Creatures, well, they are easier to force into doing ones' bidding. As are humans. Knowing the two of them, I would say it is much less likely that they will enlist the aid of plain mortals. Vampires, possibly. Shifters are also possible. But neither are probable. Zeus has always been fascinated with the minotaur, so likely one or more of those. Too far inland for sea creatures but trolls and cyclops are quite possible. Hercules is still around and he never did take to learning. So he is recruitable as he is Zeus's favorite child. They are likely to stick with large, intimidating creatures or demigods that are somewhat slowed by their size as compared to these particular humans and are not going to be very good at planning or adjusting a plan on the fly."

Devon purses his lips a moment and says, "So probably not as smart or fast as Cerberus?"

Athena inclines her head to hide a small smile, "Not by a long shot. But I would be curious to know the story behind that question."

Hades laughs, "We have been training these two to be her protectors and Cerberus loves the chase. These two are passable at this point."

Athena looks very intently at a wall to the left of her but I see her lips tremble as she holds in her own amusement.

Hera speaks, "I agree with Athena's estimation. Having been privy to all the meetings on Olympus and a number of them off site, I know he has been in frequent contact with the creatures mentioned. He has also talked with Hercules and to a few others, but they were not pleased to see him in the way that Hercules was. If I had to guess, I would say that Hercules will be the only demigod fighting there. He has been keeping the Caucasion Eagle at Prometheus' liver all this time, I imagine he can call that beast to him as well. I am certain that Prometheus would be quite grateful to the one that rid him of the bane that is the eagle eating his liver daily."

Aries nods, "You know, she could set him free. Zeus only punished him so because with fire humans were able to evolve past a point where they needed us. He needs to be seen as the center of the universe. It's why he is lacking in friends or allies. There were plenty that would be his ally, a long time ago. Zeus burned bridges over and over with his callous disregard for anyone beyond himself. The only ones to have stayed beside him were you, Hera, until now, and Demeter. She never stopped pining for him and she is quite insane." Aries notices me watching him speak and continues, "After word spread about what she did to you, I set about paying more attention to what happened in the house of Demeter. None of what I saw was good and I have kept tabs on her all this time." He turns his gaze to Hera, "It was strange to me that every time Zeus went wandering as he called it, a strange beast that looked Minotaur-like would arrive at Demeter's house. When the beast left Zeus would shortly return."

"That is interesting Aries." Hera leans forward, "Why did you not mention this before?"

"There has never been love lost between us Hera. I am still very certain that you would not actually have believed me." Aries sighs, "And that was good sense on your part. I have definitely lied to get what I want many times over."

Hera narrows her eyes, shrugs and nods, "I suppose you may be right Aries. I have let a lot of my anger at your father get in the way of everything else. I apologize son, I will try to do better."

Aries looks away, "I will try too. Maybe I could save the warring for outside the family, excepting this particular time." He runs a hand across the back of his neck, "Maybe a change in leadership will be a good thing. Perhaps this girl child of Hades and Persephone will lead all of us into better."

Charles clears his throat and holds up his phone, "We both agree, this is where she is. It is the north-east side of town, a lot of lake houses up there and most of them spend more time vacant than they do occupied. If I needed to hide out, that would be a great place for it."

Devon elbows him, "If that is where you would hide out then why did you have Fate at your place in town?"

Charles turns toward Devon and raises his brow, "Because I wasn't hiding from you. I already knew I had more resources than you and could easily overpower you." He looks over to Memré, "I was unaware of you at the time, little double threat."

Memré smiles widely and Malachi growls before she

turns to scowl at him. He shrugs and Charles turns away from the spectacle with a grin. "This is the address where we will find Fate. We have shifters—"

"Including an owl and two more wolves."

Devon splutters, "Maria? But you, you aren't a fighter."

"I have been many things beyond cook and head of this household. I don't like to fight and my form isn't always the best suited for it. But I can and will for Fate."

Athena looks on with favor at Maria, "Ah, a true daughter of Athena. I will have my eye on you little one. Charles is right, we should assess our resources and get moving. Our delay benefits him in that every minute is another for him to collect more allies."

Julian says, "I can call Maggie and have her send shifters to meet us there. She is kind of the shifter phone tree for problems. We could be on the move and know that reinforcements will follow." Charles nods his agreement and turns to face Julian, they converse quietly while Devon listens with one ear and watches us all.

I stand, "I think we have done all we can from here. Let us go reclaim our daughter and the dignity of the gods."

Charles

Twenty minutes later we have all been transported to an old barn not far from where Fate is being held. It is all I can do not to take off through the woods to go find her so when they ask for a volunteer to stake out the place, I jumped on it. I was surprised when Maria did as well. Happily, she won't slow me down and she might see something from above that I can't see.

Benny walks over to me before we can leave the barn, Rico by his side with a bag in his hand. "Hey boss, we have the ear pieces we usually use out on detail. They're all charged. They might not be so great for allowing the shifters to communicate with us, but it would allow them to hear us. Want us to pass'em out?"

"Yes! Thank you. You two are the best. Give me two, I will affix one to Maria after she changes."

They drop them in my hand and I go outside where Maria has already shifted and is waiting on a limb in a tree.

"Maria, could you come down here? I would like to attach a device to you so that I can communicate with you."

She floats to the ground landing just in front of me. Kneeling, I show her the ear piece and she cocks her head to one side. I tell her, "I thought maybe I could tie this to some feathers? Would that work?"

She bobs her head in what looks like yes and then Athena is there kneeling beside me. Maria walks directly to her and puts her head into Athena's outstretched hand. "Hand me the ear piece."

I set it carefully into her hand and she holds the hand near one side of Maria's head. I watched as it seems to dissolve and reform into an image on her feathers. Athena tells Maria, "The device will work as it should now, and when you change again it will be in your ear. You will be able to take it out just like everyone else.

Maria bobs her head and makes some burbling noises to Athena. I slip in my ear piece, "Are you ready Maria? Do you need a boost?"

They both turn their heads to look at me and though an owl's face isn't all that expressive I get the impression that she is giving me a look similar to the very unimpressed look Athena is serving up currently.

"Ok. Well, I am going to head out now. I'll let you know if I see anything." With that I am slipping through the woods, fast and silent. I changed into one of the workout uniforms we generally use for training with Cerberus and they really are amazing for the speed vampires are capable of making. I feel Fate is much closer so I slow, picking my way through the brush as I get near a cleared area. I see a group of people lounging around back on a large veranda. Pru is walking through serving them all, quiet and lips pursed. She looks more sane than I have ever seen her before today. I hear the screech of a barn owl and look up, Maria dips in a glide toward the front of the house. I make my way through the brush till I am more toward the front of the place but still off to the left in the wooded area. I don't see anything particularly spectacular as I scan the place until I look at the windows. There. It's her. She is tied to a chair and she looks tired. I hear the screech again and I look up just in time to see an eagle smash into Maria. She falls from the sky toward the woods and I race to catch her. The eagle seems to be slowly following her, unconcerned that his prey might escape. I make the leap and snatch her from the air, tucking her into the crook of my arm as I sprint away from the area. I make a really wide circle away from the barn and through some other yards before I head to the barn, as I start for the barn I speak, "Guys, I think Maria is hurt. I haven't had time to look at her but this giant fucking eagle slammed her out of the sky. I'm on my way and I have her."

My earpiece is suddenly awash with sound as it seems everyone is talking all at once. I ignore it all and put on some speed as I feel Maria's blood seeping into my suit. I make it into the barn and before I stop completely Athena has taken the owl from me and is laying her on a table. She leans in to peer at her side before waving an annoyed hand in the air, making a globe of light appear and hover over the owl. She gently moves the wing away from her body, exposing a gaping hole where the beak of the eagle pierced her. A single tear falls from Athena's eye as she places a hand over the wound and one on Maria's little owl head. Her hands glow and the owl burbles weakly. The glow intensifies then stops entirely.

Athena takes her hands away as the little owl gets to its feet then blooms into a sparkling white light that moves and shifts, finally leaving Maria sitting naked on the table. Athena reaches for Maria at the same time as Maria wraps her arms around her. I hear a muffled thank you. I turn to find Hades at that point and the bastard is standing next to me. I almost flinched. His slow smile says he knows but I don't think anyone else saw it. "Come on, now that you have seen her healed you need to report to Persephone and Aries. Athena will be busy a moment yet, she has a very soft spot for owls."

Toward the back of the barn is where everyone else is congregated. Aries and Persephone are looking over a map of the neighborhood and discussing how far the human shield needs to extend. They stop speaking as we approach, Persephone asks, "What did you find?"

I tell her as succinctly as possible, the gods demand descriptions of the ones lounging on the veranda out back.

Aries nods when I finish, "It isn't as bad as it could be. No giants. Obviously the Caucasion Eagle has been called in. I am pretty certain that is what hit the little owl Athena is currently fawning over." He looks at Persephone, "That bird is going to come out of this with armored feathers. Or something. She has never been able to leave her favorites without extra defenses."

Persephone shrugs, "Whatever gets my daughter back and those two in Tartarus."

A little more discussion and the plan is decided. Night has fallen and we are on our way back out. Maria now has a sword and shield, but she will take flight once the eagle has been taken out. A few dozen more shifters have arrived. Aries and Athena have given us all our orders and now we all walk into the woods. Devon and Julian are with me, Julian is a pretty damn big wolf. Seamus, Ryna, Ajah, Rico, and Benny are to the left and right of us. I can't see anyone else, but all of us were sent around toward the front with the mission to free Fate and kill that fucking bird. We move fast till we get close enough to see the lights from the house. As we get into place I hear a bloodcurdling scream and shouts, "I think that's our cue. Let's get our girl." We rush toward the house, still low to the ground and quiet.

$$\mathit{Sixteen}$$

FATE

They have been arriving all day. All these demigods, none of them stronger than most members of the magical community. The one they call Heracles is dumb. The sliding glass door leading to the back veranda is hard for him. Demeter threw some designs on the glass just so he would stop walking through it. Pru hates him, I'm not sure if that is because he is so dumb or because he keeps trying to grope her.

It doesn't matter. She slipped a knife into my hands hours ago and I have the ropes hanging on by a thread. I am not really worried about the demigods, but I am worried about the way Zeus is eating up my power. I don't know how to stop that and I know the plan is to kill me. I have been working to slow the drain as much as I can, considering I am just guessing. It seems to be working, I don't feel nearly so tired as I did earlier.

I saw an eagle arrive earlier, the thing is huge. I didn't know they made them that big. I think it could possibly do some actual damage to me. I heard it scream earlier, Zeus and Demeter smiled. They do seem really smug over the strange wolves they have hidden in the woods. They are odd. They remind me of shifters, or maybe something like Cerberus. I don't know what to think about them. There had to be twenty or so. They do the bidding of Demeter but not willingly, I don't think. They look miserable.

I can feel Devon and Charles are near, and have been for most of the day. Charles was so close I could smell him earlier, around the time that blasted eagle shrieked. He doesn't feel injured, I hope no one else is. I know they will be coming for me soon, I strain my hearing to the limit, listening for any little thing that might tell me they are here. The fools are outside drinking it up, celebrating with Zeus and Demeter over the capture of me. Assholes. I hear an ear piercing scream, that's my cue. Pru runs out of the back of the house as I break the ropes. She stops, wary. We both hear the sound of fighting out back, "Pru, just leave. Pop on out of here and go away. You don't have to be part of this. I can protect you from her finding you ever again, if you want that."

Pru looks out the glass doors as we hear the howls from the woods, looking back to me she nods once. I take some of my precious power reserve and make her invisible to the both of them. "It is done, they will never be able to see you in any way ever again. Go, find a way to be happy Pru."

The front door bursts open and Pru disappears. I turn, hands coming up and ready to fight when I see Devon and Charles leading the way to me. They grab me up in a tight embrace, and a giant wolf jams his head against my side, I set a hand on his head, "Julian?" The wolf licks my hand and grins at me. "Who else is with you?"

Benny answers, "About fifteen shifters, a few gods, and us."

"Shit. We have to get out there, they had reinforcements hiding in the woods. Try not to kill them, I don't think they want to be here. But get that fucking eagle, it is Zeus' pet."

Seamus says, "It got Maria earlier, I think getting it is definitely the plan." He puts a finger in his ear and seems to be mumbling at his ear.

I want to ask if Maria is all right but the glass behind us shatters as Heracles walks through it. I spot my mother in the crowd, fighting one of her sisters. She throws a ball of darkness at me, it hits me in the chest and the drain stops. Cut off like it never happened. With a grin I send a shot of energy at Heracles blowing him back out the door. "Let's go even some odds!" I take off running through the empty space recently vacated by that brute. The strange wolves are everywhere. Nipping at people, they don't seem to care what side they bite. Julian leaps past me, taking out a wolf that was heading to bite Ryna. Her and the tiger beside her are fighting Pelasgas, he is lightning fast and tough as nails, but still bleeding from those two. He isn't the one I want though. I see my father dealing with Demeter, she is attacking him, but I'm not looking for her either. I move through the fight, throwing shots occasionally to help my people. I see Maria fighting side by side with a beautiful woman that I think might be Athena. Zeus is the one I want though, I want that bastard dead. I turn in a slow circle, I am still not seeing him when I feel hands grab me from behind pulling me up against a body that smells of putrid rot and decay. Finally, Zeus. He puts a knife to my throat as he shouts, amplified across the clearing. The fighting freezes, with the exception of the wolf that Julian had already sent flying through the air landing on yet another. Zeus is no longer disguised and the horro of his visage is reflected on all the faces before me.

Zeus tells them, "Whoever put the block on her, take it off now, or I'll cut her where it won't grow back!"

I keep my body lax, as I look at the faces of everyone I love. All of them here to save me. I love every single one of them so damn much. I watch in horror as the eagle slams into Seamus, ripping his head off as he hits the ground. Marina throws herself into the air, changing as she flies at the eagle still screeching its triumph. Her talons sink deep into its face, then she pushes herself back into the air, a sickly sucking, tearing sound as she pulls the eagle's eye out with her. Ajah in her tiger form lands on the back of the thrashing eagle, bearing it to the ground where a screaming Ryna slams her blade through the eagle's neck, severing it and sending gouts of blood flying.

I look back at Devon and Charles, seeing the fear of my death reflected in their eyes as I listen to Ryna mourning her brother. I can't let them go through that. I wrap myself in a shield and at the same time I wrap Zeus in one to keep him from disappearing. Lifting my foot I stomp on his instep and use my power to help me flip him over my head and onto the ground in front of me. I can hear screams around me but I don't dare take my eyes off this bastard. I send his knife flying as my own flames flare and suddenly I know, I am the Goddess of Blessed Death and Beginnings. I reach down into Zeus, past the filth and muck that is his physical form, taking hold of the pestilence that is his spirit I snatch it out of his body.

He screams at me at I hold his spirit up in the air, his spirit beats at my hand. "How dare you! Insolent child! You put me back! What do you think you are doing! You are playing at things you don't understand!"

"I know exactly what I am doing! I am ending this. Choose. The silence of obliteration or the prison of Tartarus. You will never again be left free to destroy lives."

"I choose neither! You have no power over me weak girl! Demeter! Help your beloved!"

To my right I hear Demeter struggling to get to us, I don't know who has her or if they will be able to hold her. "Tartarus then, because I want you to suffer the way you have made others suffer." I enclose his spirit in a box and disappear the box to Tartarus. No one will be able to open it until I allow it and Zeus has no powers as I stripped them away from him when I snatched him from his body. I turn to deal with Demeter, just in time to see Hera punch her in the temple, knocking her out.

I am still mad and I encase Demeter in a box as well, disappearing her to Tartarus. I may face a punishment of my own for this but those two will never again hurt people for their own gain or pleasure.

The fighting is at a stand still, the only sounds in the clearing are those of Ryna's grief and Ajah growling at anyone that draws near Ryna. It looks like she did allow Malachi in, as he is grieving with her. The strange wolves move to circle me and before I can blink Devon, Charles, and Julian are between me and the wolves. One of the wolves changes, becoming a half-starved, naked, man who immediately kneels before me, "Please don't send us with them. We had no choice." The change ripples through their rank and they all look equally abused as they kneel. I am surrounded by them and their pain permeates the air.

"Rise, please. Get yourselves dressed and be at ease. I won't be sending you to Tartarus."

Hera says to my mother, "See, she acts the part already. She is the right choice."

I look over at the woman in surprise, "The right choice for what?"

Seventeen

FATE

Devon turns to me, "They decided you should be queen."

"Queen? Of what?"

Charles is the one that laughs, "Of the Gods sweetheart. They decided it was time for a new leader and that you are the one for the job."

"What? I've been kidnapped twice in the past year and I just ripped a god from his body before sending him and his lover to Tartarus. Does that honestly sound like the kind of level-headed decisions that make for queen?"

The man that was holding Demeter back steps forward saying, "Hi. Aries here. Nice to meet you. Finally. Actually, those are the actions of a woman that should be queen. Your actions were fair and honestly, I would have sent Zeus into the great oblivion that would have ensured he will never return for my head. You might think on that yourself. Just good business practice to eliminate enemies such as him. I digress. You would make a fine queen, if you choose to do so. You are sickeningly fair minded and you don't seem possessed by vengeance or anything else that would make you easy to control. That is a shame really, but probably for the best."

Hera steps forward, clearing her throat, "It was my idea. Having been the wife of the ruler for so long, I have had ample time to observe what does and does not make a good ruler. I would not. I am angry, jealous, and I have held grudges for a long time. Often against one that was wronged just as much as I. We, all of the gods, need a ruler that will lead us to be better than we have."

My mind races, mostly with the thought that I don't know if I can handle all this. Can I live up to what these people are expecting from me? Is there any way in all the world that I could possibly be fit to be queen of the gods? "I. I really need to think about this. Could I have some time to think about this?"

Hera narrows her eyes and purses her lips, "Yes. But not long. There are those who would usurp the role and we do not need a war among us. As it is, there will be those that will cry that this was an act of war. You may have three days. We can keep this quiet for that long. Aries, Athena; gather up the demigods. We will put them in the basement. They can sit there till she makes her choice. Three days. No more. And then you must choose." She looks to my mother, "Make sure she understands just how much is at stake for her personally. You know how they view threats."

Hera disappears and a blond man walks over to me. He takes my hand, "Fate, whatever you decide, know that you are suited for this role. I believe you could lead all of us into being better. Some of us have a lot to work on, and even more to learn. We need someone not bound in the ways of old, someone that believes in the autonomy of each human. Your parents may well be the best of us, but even they have their faults and ways in which they are locked into the past. The fact that none of us realized, or even thought to question why Demeter would work so hard for some random beast we were never allowed to meet when Zeus has always been her love… I think it illustrates our issues well. For now, I go back to my sea. If you should need me, call my name at flowing water, I will hear you."

My face crinkles, "Well, I would but I don't know your name."

He laughs, "I am Poseidon. Your parents have failed you by not ensuring you know each of us by sight and energy signature."

"Shut up Poseidon." My mother crosses her arms over her chest, "There hasn't been enough time. I taught her the important things first, she kills just fine. Zeus's remains over there stand testament to that."

He fades into nothing as he says with a smile, "I suppose you did."

Aries comes to my side, slipping his arm in mine he says, "Walk with me, I will introduce you to the Goddess of Love, Aphrodite."

I walk with him to a woman standing over the body of one of my mother's sisters. I recognize them only because they resemble her so much. The woman has been watching the body intently the entire time and leans down to pull a knife from her chest as we approach. As she straightens she says, "I always try to make sure they are completely dead before I remove the weapon. The poison would continue to do its job but I feel like keeping the knife in their heart until it is sure just speeds the process."

"I agree. Aphrodite, this is Fate. Our newest goddess and possible queen. Fate, this is Aphrodite."

She shoves a bloody hand toward me and I reach out to shake it, belatedly realizing that I still have some Zeus on my hand. She seems unbothered as she gives my hand a solid pump before releasing it. "Very nice to meet you Fate." She leans forward and peers into my eyes, "Oh, there is a lot of love in this one. And passion for days. She will be a good one to watch, especially if she collects half of the lovers her mother has set up for her. The wolf looks especially fun, let me know how that goes. I may have to go find one of my own."

I tip my head to one side, "Are you, do you know who all the lovers my mother has set up for me are?"

She laughs loud and long, "I do. I know all the matches of each and every person or god. That's why I was always so puzzled about Demeter being with some strange beast, she loved Zeus. I suppose it makes sense now, knowing they are one and the same."

"Well that is awkward. You aren't going to share that information, are you?"

"Oh no, I would much rather watch you stumble into them. Makes things so much more interesting for me. Besides, after Helen I lost my taste for interfering. That one spiraled so bad…"

"I actually get that. Well, it was very nice meeting the two of you. But, my lovers are quite restless over there and my parents really seem to want to talk to me as well."

Aphrodite barks a laugh, "I bet they do. They don't really want you to accept the job. It is dangerous. Other factions will want to take it from you. But your parents will stand with you and they are a formidable pair. Also the truest love match I had ever seen when they found each other. You would do well to take the job. No point in having all the bullshit and none of the perks. It was nice meeting you. I look forward to seeing what you decide." She evaporates into sea mist, leaving a salty spray behind.

Aries laughs, a low rumbly sound that causes flutters in my belly and growls from behind me. "I will take my leave as well, darling Fate. Before I am faced with fighting all of your lovers." He takes my hand in his, drawing it to his lips he places a light kiss on my knuckles before he pops out of sight.

Julian shoves his head under my other hand, licking my fingers with his rough tongue. I slide my hand back over his head and through his fur. "Come, let's go talk with my very patient parents." I look to Ryna and Malachi as I walk to my parents. Ajah has calmed and is being held very firmly by a distraught Ryna while Malachi is holding tightly to Memré. I am so glad she is being a friend to him, she could use a male friend, and more but I can't push her into that with my memories of how much I hated to be pushed into a relationship when I was not ready still so vibrant in my mind.

I can't help but wonder if my parents will be upset with me for what I did to Zeus and Demeter. They are my mother's parents and my father's siblings, which is its own brand of twisted but whatever. As I draw near to them they close the gap and enfold me in a hug between the two of them, I feel the tears flowing from both of them as they hold me tight.

I enjoy the moment for as long as they need it. I know reality will intrude upon us all too soon. They release me, though they do not move more than a couple steps away.

"We are so glad to have you safe and free." Persephone looks around at the battlefield, still littered with the bodies of demigods, a few wolves, an eagle, and Seamus. "I know that Hera is pushing for you to accept the role of queen, but you don't have to do that. You can walk away from it."

Hades shakes his head, "Love, you know she can't. From the moment it was spoken out loud the option to walk away with no consequences evaporated. Like so much dew in the morning sun. The knowledge that she would be supported as queen is out there. Her best chance is to be queen of her own choice, instead of winning it by defeating those who would attack her for the potential threat she poses. Apollo is not going to sit idly by with Zeus gone. You know he has always thought that the sun god," his eyes roll even as he spits out the words, "should be king of the gods. He has always been insufferable and ruthless, when no one is looking."

Tears slip down my mother's face as she listens to my father. "He is not wrong, though I would make it so. Apollo isn't the only one. The Titans were set free a few centuries ago, with the oath that they would not try to rule again so long as Zeus was king. Cronus will want to lead again. He can't be allowed. His violence and treachery knew no bounds. As much as I hate this, you don't have much choice. Whatever you decide they will still be after you."

My jaw is hanging open and I shut it with a snap. Fucking hell. The Titans? Apollo? "Couldn't I just swear, take an oath, that I will never seek the throne?"

My father shakes his head, "No, my sweet. They will not trust you because they would continually be seeking a way around their oath, and they cannot believe that you or anyone else would be any different."

"But, I don't want to be queen. I just want to live my life, try to adjust to it because it is wild these days. I don't need more thrown at me!"

Devon and Charles step up beside me, one to each side

and each slips an arm around me. Julian, still a wolf, settles himself at my feet. It is oddly comforting having that huge fuzzy beast leaning into my legs. My mother and father lean into each other, she says, "We would spare you this if there were any other way. If we thought it would work, we would find a way to keep all of this from you. Unfortunately, anything we did would only prolong the eventual outcome. I want to tell you to walk away," my father gives her a squeeze as her voice catches, "but it will ultimately find you. Your best course of action will be in standing tall, accepting the mantle of queen, and knowing that you are meant for this. You are strong enough for this, and your triumph will be a win for the world. There is no one better suited for the job than you."

I draw a shaky breath, "And no one is upset that I killed Zeus?"

"What? No!" My father laughs, "He deserved to die and would have died soon anyway. That is why they were so desperate for their plan to go through. He couldn't use just any body, it had to be that of a god. By the time he found out that it was possible to steal the body of a god, heh, he wasn't able to create a new one himself. Demeter couldn't find a god to have sex with her, but I believe that was mostly for lack of trying. She never really wanted anyone but Zeus. Once you killed him, I became privy to his entire life, and he is so much more horrible than any of us could have imagined. You have done the world a favor. And, our little Goddess of the Blessed Death and Blessed

Beginnings, you are absolutely made for this. You have lived as a human, multiple times. You, better than any of us, understand what it is to live with a limited life span. With the knowledge of just what it is like to be in the power of someone else. I know you have been working to set up a foundation to do more for the magical community. As the queen over all the gods, you can set the laws that we live by. You can effect changes for the better from the very top. This is an opportunity to do good in a way that may not have been possible before."

I pause in my misery at the idea that I could effect some real change. I am definitely trying to wallow in the misery of the idea of so much responsibility, this is huge. Dad is right though, the responsibility is there but I would also have the power to do a lot of really good things. "And you would be there for me, both of you?" I look around, "What about you all? Devon? Charles? Julian? Natasha? Billy? Memré? Ajah? Everyone that came to my aid today? What are your thoughts? You are all my family, my loves. What I do affects you. How do you feel about this?"

Devon and Charles look at each other, shrug, and Charles speaks for them, "We are all in wherever you go. That won't change. I think Juli down there at your feet would agree."

Julian sits up and pushes his head into my belly, "Is that an agreement? Shake your head yes or no. I need clarity sir."

He leans back and grins, his wolfish smile is the cutest thing, and then he very firmly moves his head up and down a few times before shoving it back at my belly. I pat his head before I step back from them to turn and see what everyone else feels. Natasha and Billy give me a thumbs up. Memré looks over at me from where she is still comforting Malachi, she shakes her head yes. Ryna and Ajah seem to be in some sort of communication. Ryna's face is streaked with blood, tears, and snot, as is Ajah's fur. Ryna nods once and then turns to me, "We are with you."

Malachi lifts his head briefly, "I am with you." I have the distinct feeling that his support is based on Ryna's, but I am ok with that. I barely know him.

Maria is standing still next to the woman she fought next to, "I am with you. Athena, supports this as well and has adopted me into her fold so it would appear that I will be a part of that world whether I willed it or no."

Athena laughs and then turns her attention to me, "Will you stand and fight or will you run away?"

The sudden severity of her voice is startling. I square my shoulders, "I will fight."

She claps her hands together, "Excellent! It is decided then! I will see you all at the coronation." She disappears after that pronouncement and I am left with the realization that I did just agree to become queen and it was more because I didn't like the implication of cowardice than because I was ready to accept it.

I see the abused wolves standing off to the side and I know I can't leave them here. Would they even survive? Could they keep themselve hidden from rest of the world? I look down at Julian, "Can you, John, and Steve lead them to the house while staying out of sight? No one in this town is going to be ok with large groups of wolves wandering openly through town." Julian nods, and two wolves leap over to land near him, I recognize Steve and John. I follow them over to the others, "I know you are all tired. I will get you fed and find somewhere to put you that will be safe. But first, you must change and follow these three in smaller groups to my home." I turn, "Maria, will you fly home and get food sorted? Order more, or send Sheri and Nicki out if you need supplies."

She nods as she changes and takes flight. I turn in time to see the change ripple through the crowd in front of me. Steve moves off to one side while John moves off to another, the wolves that just changed begin to sort themselves into three groups. I am horrified at the way they look. Their fur is matted, their wolves are emaciated. I look down to Julian, "Are you all able to communicate with each other?" He shakes his wolfy head yes, "Ok, all of you make sure you are not seen. See what you can find out about them. I need to know what they need to become self sufficient." He stands and licks the side of my face. "Ugh! Julian!" He gives me a wolfish grin before he leaps off to the side and takes off. The group waiting in front of him turns and follows his lead. I wipe the saliva off my face as I watch the other two groups follow suit. Devon and Charles step up beside me, "He's going to stay, isn't he?" Devon says as he pulls me close. Charles laughs, "We were going to tell you we approve of him but you disappeared before we had the chance."

"Well, in that case I feel better about telling you both that yes, I do plan to keep him. I, to me he feels like one of you. Like you both did when I first saw you. Less creepy than you were then Charles." He chuckles ruefully, "But he still feels like one of you. I can no more say no to him than I could to either of you."

Eighteen

It has been a week since I agreed to be crowned queen. In that week the small semblance of order I thought I had has disappeared. My house is in an uproar, there are two to three packs worth of wolves living in the barracks I placed out back. I had to create them relatively quickly after I had them led here with the promise that I would help them. To their credit, they are really amazing people. Incredibly subservient and I don't know how to help them out of that. It is great that they want to help, but I worry that they will be taken advantage of and possibly trapped by someone else less scrupulous.

Perhaps I could get them a therapist? If nothing else I will keep them with me, and make sure they are safe for the remainder of their lives. On that note, I need to get out of this bed. The guys left me to sleep knowing that I have been going nonstop for the better part of the week. I don't need much sleep as a goddess, but after a week of catnaps I needed a few solid hours. I pad to the bathroom and take care of business there. Refreshed, I step out into the bedroom. Hmm, I think someone has taken my robe off to be washed. I may as well get dressed for the day. I head for the closet and begin the search for something to wear today. Now that I have accepted my role as Goddess of Blessed Death and Beginnings, I hear the prayers. It is a hum in my head all the time unless I block it out. People begging for a death to come or for a new beginning. I grant the ones that have lived their lives and are only suffering. But the ones that are suffering and there is a way out, them I send a new beginning. I can't control what they do with it. Perhaps they will end up back where they were when they begged for death. I find a dress, red and fitted. It has a nice v-neck that does magnificent things for my cleavage. I turn to find some underthings and run directly into Julian.

His strong arms wrap around me to stop me from falling on my naked ass. I find myself pressed against his chest, our bodies snugged together like they were made for each other. I look up into eyes that are dark with passion, his lips are slightly parted as he looks down at me. Dropping the dress I raise up on my tip toes, "Now you've caught me, what are you going to do?"

He crushes his lips to mine, he smells like woodsmoke and dark forests long forgotten. My arms are trapped at my sides as he lifts me to his height, I wrap my legs around his hips. There is nothing that turns me on more than a strong man picking me up like it was nothing. Vampires and shifters, oh how I love them! I feel his cock straining his jeans and he breaks the kiss, "I need to set you down for a moment."

I giggle as I unwrap my legs, letting them dangle until he sets me gently on the ground. The instant I have my balance he works to snatch his own clothing off and I step back to get the entire view. In the short time he has been here Julian and I haven't had any time alone. He gets his shirt up over his head and I say, "Slower please. I want to enjoy the show." His body is amazing. The muscles on this man, he could be in a calendar. He grins at me when he sees me checking out his chest, so I decide to push things further. As his hands move to the button on his jeans I tell him, "Stop. Let me do this. You just… keep your hands behind your back." He inhales deeply as I step up to him, whispering, "I want to explore you." I run my hands over his pecs and he shivers, his breathing is becoming more ragged by the moment. I trail my hands over his washboard abs, feeling them contract at my touch. My hands at his waist, I unbutton his pants and gently slip my hand between him and his zipper. He sucks air as my hand rubs against him and I lower the zip, freeing him. I push his jeans down his legs and straighten, allowing him a moment to kick them off to the side. He growls and grabs me by the waist, I squeal in delight as he lifts me into the air, bringing my breasts level with his mouth. My squeal turning to a moan of ecstasy as his mouth and tongue go to work on my nipples, sucking hard and then circling the nubs with his tongue.

I wrap my legs around his body as he starts to kiss his way up my neck, stopping to bite me in a few spots. As he lowers me his cock meets with my dripping pussy and my hips rock involuntarily. He growls into my neck, biting me lightly as he impales me. I almost cum right then. He whispers in my ear as he moves his hands to cup my ass, "Touch yourself, I won't last long this time. I have been waiting too long to get to you." I feel my core quiver at his whispered words and I move one hand from gripping his shoulders to between us, pressed against that glorious bundle of nerves. I feel his teeth sink into the sweet spot where shoulder and neck join again as he begins to piston himself into me. The feel of his cock hammering me as my fingers rub that bundle of nerves have me leaping over the edge within moments and he follows me over, slamming into me one more time to hold himself buried in me.

Our breathing still ragged I tap his shoulder and unlock my legs, starting to swing them down when he convulses, "Stop! OH gods! Stay still for just a little longer. Too much…"

I laugh but swing my legs back into place, and he lets out a deep sigh. He moves one hand at a time so he is supporting my legs. Feeling a little wicked I wiggle and he moans before he smacks my ass. I laugh and he says, "I think I can do this now." He lifts me up off his cock which is still hard. I uncross my legs and he lowers me to the floor, releasing his neck once I have my footing.

"Care for a quick shower while you are here brightening my day?"

"I think I need one."

Ten minutes later, freshly showered we go back to the closet and I pick up my dress. Thank goodness for materials that don't wrinkle up for laying on the floor a bit. I grab some panties and a bra from the drawers. Slipping those on I find Julian watching me, "Enjoying the show?"

He nods, "Mostly just memorizing the clothing so I know how best to have my way with you."

I laugh as I slip the dress over my head, I hear Charles saying, "You really have that little experience with women's clothing that you need to memorize her clothing?"

"No. I just assume she prefers I don't rip them off."

I am laughing as I get my dress sorted and Charles wraps his arms around me from behind, pressing a kiss to my neck. I shiver with the longing for him, I never seem able to have enough of them. He smiles and then lifts his head, "Coffee is waiting downstairs love. I came to wake you but it appears Juli beat me to it this morning."

"Hmm, no. I was awake when he arrived. He just beat you to morning sex. Now I need coffee. Come gentlemen, escort me downstairs please." Charles slips my arm through his and Julian steps up on the other side to follow his example.

Charles tells me as we walk, "Your parents are here.

They said they need to talk with you and prepare you for things. That you should have information this time that you didn't, couldn't have before you were first activated."

"That is a relief actually. I feel like I have been blindsided a lot since Devon walked into my library. It will be nice to have some expectation of how things should go."

They escort me to the door of a sitting room, inside my parents are conversing with Maria as she sets a small buffet on the coffee table before them. Devon is seated opposite my parents on a loveseat and I take the seat next to him, leaving Julian and Charles to take the chairs on either side.

We all help ourselves to Maria's breakfast version of tapas, her food is not to be missed for anything. I help myself to coffee with my food, as I am still very much in love with it, whether or not I really need it. Silence reigns for the first few minutes as we all just enjoy the food. I set my plate on the table next to me and lean back to enjoy my coffee. Shortly my mom does the same, though she is drinking tea. She clears her throat and says, "We couldn't prepare you for becoming a goddess until the change was begun. We are with you now and we can prepare you for the coronation. As well as what being queen of the gods entails. First, you will need to choose your court. It is recommended that the members of your court be immortal, simply for the fact that time slips by so fast and one day you will be heartbroken to find your trusted person will pass soon. We have all experienced it, the mortal lifespan is so short when you live, effectively, forever." She sips her tea and looks away, lips pressed together. "You are able to grant immortality to those you deem worthy or needful. While there is not a restriction on how many, I do urge caution in whom you grant this gift to, as there is only one way to remove it."

Sipping my coffee I think about that. "Wait, do you mean…?"

She nods, "Death. Yes. That is the only way. Immortal only means they will not age, not that they cannot die. Much like your vampire friends, they are just more resistant to death. In addition, some people do not wish for immortality. We must respect their wishes no matter how we wish them to stay."

I look around the room and a question occurs to me, "What, um, what happens to a vampire that drinks from a god regularly?"

I feel my cheeks heating as my dad narrows his eyes, looking at Charles and Devon. Then he laughs, "They will generally become faster, smarter, and possibly over the course of a few hundred years or so develop some small powers. Beyond that, it probably endears them to you."

I laugh as the guys relax and Julian snickers. Devon and Charles shoot him dirty looks but he just grins. My mom cuts them off with a look, "That question out of the way, the coronation. There is an entire ceremony, most of it is just a show. The important part is when the challenge questions are asked. The first will be who supports this woman as ruler. The second will be who challenges this woman's right to rule. That is where things get tricky. As

Aries mentioned, it is very likely that Apollo will want to challenge. That being the case, you will have the option of fighting him yourself or choosing a champion. While I do think you could take him because he is not in fighting form these days, I advise choosing a champion. The reason for this is that he has had centuries to learn techniques that you will not have a defense against and you don't have time to pursue the training that you would need. I would suggest Aries, Athena, Poseidon, Hekate, or your father. Do not choose me, I will take his soul from his body and set it to blaze in the middle of Tartarus. It really would not be good form."

Devon, Charles, and Julian are all watching my mother with jaws hanging. My father is laughing and I am grinning like a fool, my mom is such a badass. This is wildly inspiring. The guys manage to recover as Devon says to me, "All this time we were worried about what your father might do to us and he isn't the one we should be worried about, is he?"

My grin never slips as I tell him, "I don't think he is."

Mom replies, "Of the two of us, I am the more violent and blood-thirsty. Though admittedly, I have less experience at that than your father does. I missed out on some wars. Moving on, once the fight is done and the loser removed to a… secure location. We finish the coronation and move on to the ball. There will be dancing and food and lots of polite speaking with your new subjects. Most of whom will be trying to get your agreement to some scheme or other. You will need to be at the top of your game which means no alcohol of any kind." She points at each of the guys in turn, "It will be your responsibility to ensure that her drinks remain pure. More than one of the minor gods, and some of the major ones, will have nothing against drugging you. I will gift you each with a set of contacts that you will wear and they will allow you to see any additives. Whether it is alcohol, drugs, or magic. The contacts will dissolve two days after they are put in. That should get you all through coronation night and a full day plus after that."

I cringe, "Really? They would stoop so low? I obviously have a lot of work to do. I would ask how they thought this was ok but after meeting my grandfather and feeling incredibly grateful that his dick had rotted off before I met him… I think I have an idea."

My mother lifts one shoulder briefly and continues, "You will have contacts as well, but you will be distracted and should not be the first line of defense in that regard. Once the ball ends, and you can set a specific end point. I would. You don't want Dionysus think this is going to be a week long party like Zeus had after he defeated Cronus and crowned himself. We need to have a dress created for you, well, a few dresses. Unless you would prefer a suit of some sort?"

"Um…I want a dress, but what kind of dress does one wear to their coronation? I guess it needs to be pretty extra?"

Hades laughs, "Extra, yes. That is a way to describe it. You should have seen your mother when she was crowned.

It was a relatively small gathering but she chose a dress that stunned and left no one in doubt that she ruled the Underworld."

Persphone takes his hand, "Oh love, you say the sweetest things." She leans over and kisses him gently on the lips, sitting back she turns back to us, "Your dress will need to do the same. I am going to call Arachne. She is the very best."

"Arachne? Wait, wasn't she turned into a spider or something?"

My father chuckles, "Yes. But that is where the myths diverge from reality. She requested to be protected from all the suitors that would not leave her alone. She just wanted to create. She was not interested in any sort of romantic entanglement and even less interested in being owned. She begged for a release that would allow her to do what she loved without all the pressure from the men. So Athena granted her an alternate form that would scare all the suitors away and her suitors made her into an overly proud woman that was punished by her patron goddess. Athena also gifted her immortality because she felt the world would be less without such talent. Arachne has been happy ever since. Now she lives in the open as an ace person? Is that the right word? I think it is."

"It is Hades, you got it right." My mother smiles adoringly at him, "She is the best. And the rap the myths gave her is utter garbage. I will go see her shortly and send her to you. She helped me with the dress I needed and she will help you. She will understand the gravity of the situation and design something you will slay in. I think we will go there now. We have discussed the important things here, everything else is trivia. You will be queen, so any etiquette that people want to follow won't apply to you."

"Oh thank fuck for that. I am awful at all the ridiculous etiquette rules created just to differentiate classes. I look forward to meeting Arachne, she sounds amazing." I stand and walk around the table to hug my parents before they pop off to visit with their old friend. "Thank you, both of you. I love you so much and I am so grateful to know you."

My mom hugs me extra tight, "And we are so grateful to finally get to know you darling daughter. You are so much more than we could have hoped for." Releasing me, they disappear.

I wipe away the little tears in the corners of my eyes. I never expected to hear those words from parents and it makes me emotional in the best way. Devon comes over and enfolds me in his embrace. I snuggle in, happy to accept the comfort. "I guess we need to gather the house together. We all have decisions to make. I assume you three will be part of my court. Oh!" I straighten to look at Julian, "You are the only one in here that isn't immortal. Do you want to be? I mean, I want you to be but, it is still your choice."

He sighs in relief, "I do. I didn't want to ask and seem grasping but I kind of wanted you to want me to as well. Yes, I want to spend a thousand lifetimes with you, however that looks."

Charles chuckles, "I want to make fun of you here Juli, but truth is, I would feel the same. You get a pass. This time."

Devon looks down at me, "Why don't we walk to the dining room while these two gather everyone else?"

"Sounds great. If you two don't mind?" I say, looking at Charles and Julian. They say they don't mind and leave to find people. I start to move away from Devon and he tightens his arms to keep me there. I look up with a grin, "Sir, we are expected for a meeting?"

"I know, but I haven't had a chance to kiss you yet this morning."

"Oh, well," I press myself against him as I raise up on my toes, "we must correct this oversight." I put my arms around his neck and press my lips to his, the contact ignites us both and the kiss deepens. Long minutes later I break the kiss, breathing ragged. "We have to go do things. Meeting things. Important discussions."

He growls in frustration, "We are finishing this later."

"Agreed."

Fate

Devon and I walk slowly to the dining room, arm in arm. I ask him how he is doing with all these changes and he answers, "Better than I thought I would. I was prepared to be really angry and hurt over the addition of other men to our relationship. Over having to deal with the other demands on your time. But really, I wasn't. And that kind of messed me up for a little bit. Because I felt like I should be, you know?"

"I do. But I noticed you and Charles are actually pretty good together, and that happened fast. I was suspicious for a minute that you two were planning to go off and fight in secret."

He laughs, "I think it was a possibility at first, but neither of us wanted to give up the time spent with you. Plus, it seems like someone is always trying to kill you. I have never seen someone so nice with so many people trying to end them. I kind of thought that once we got Charles, back before he kidnapped you, that once that was resolved the worst would be over. Maude trying to kill you, that was not so bad because it just scared us for a moment and then you ended her. You being kidnapped by the king of gods… That was terrifying. I didn't know how we would get you back. I think Charles was hanging on by a thread much like me. Julian, he was trying to keep his feelings to himself. But I think the bond between you and him was already forming because he just seemed like part of the team. That is why we kept him with us, to put him with one of the other groups, it felt wrong."

"I like that. I like that it is all just working so well between the three of you. I have another thing I am concerned about."

"Oh?"

"Yes. The wolves. The new ones, I haven't had time to be around them, but I have seen the three of you with them. What is your opinion of them? Do you think they can be aided into independence? Or have they been too abused, too hurt? Do they maybe just need a little time to adjust?"

He sighs, "I don't think there is an easy answer to that. I think some would be able to be ushered into independence but without the group they would falter. At the same time I don't know if they would be capable of taking care of the group either. Maybe get some professionals to work with them toward independence and also prepare to care for them, at least partially for so long as they live."

We enter the dining room to find we are the first to arrive. The guys must be taking it slow rounding everyone up.

"I hate that they have been so abused, and by my family. I will do whatever it takes to ensure they live out the rest of their lives happy and healthy. If that means we keep them with us and put them to work so they feel useful, then that is what happens." Devon walks me to the head of the table and pulls out the chair for me. I sit down just as some of the bodyguards walk in and Devon takes the chair to the right. I greet them and ask Owen how his family is doing.

"Fate, they are doing amazing now. None of us realized how much it affected us knowing that the neighbors wanted us gone and the owner of the property was just as shitty. My mom smiles now. My brothers are doing well in school for the first time in too long. I don't know if I could have made this happen without you. We are in your debt."

"You absolutely are not! Your debt was paid in full every time you put your life on the line for me, if anything, I owe you. I am just glad your family is doing so well."

Everyone else has filed in as we talked, Julian and Charles taking the two seats to the left of me. Charles manages to get the seat closest to me and throws a smug grin at Julian who shrugs and returns a satisfied grin. Charles' brows drop as he scowls at Julian.

Trying not to laugh I clear my throat, "Ok, now that we are all here I need to tell you some things about the coming coronation. So first, I am going to need to spend a lot more time in Olympus than here. Anyone not ok with that, absolutely can work solely from here. Second, I have to form a court. The people on the court, and preferably my body-guards as well, will all need to be immortal," I see faces fall and I rush to tell them the rest, "I can grant that to any that are willing. Anyone that is not, will simply continue to work for me here and will have employment with a hefty retirement package for the rest of their lives or as long as they choose to work here. The retirement package is yours even if you leave from here to work for someone else. I also need to let you know, this will put you at considerably more risk. Especially as I work to sort out priorities in Olympus. Immortality does not mean you cannot die. It means you will not age into death. Your body will not grow old and die. All that said, you are welcome to ask any questions you have. I will answer them to the best of my ability and seek out the answers to any I don't know."

Owen leans forward, "I want to go and I want the

immortality. Keeping you safe is a joy and my mother will be really happy to know that I am keeping this job for life. She won't mind that I am elsewhere a lot as long as I call her sometimes. I'm in."

Natasha says, "I will need to be here some for my other duties but I am happy to be part of your court if you want me. I think I am already effectively immortal with the whole vampire thing. Plus, I like my job. Going to hire a lot more people to take over the running of the foundation. And I am fully planning to add my coronation dress to the expenses. Because it is going to be expensive."

I laugh, "Good. I wouldn't have it any other way. But hold off on dress shopping. My mother is talking to the best, maybe when she gets in touch she will be willing to create dresses for all of us."

Natasha nods as Memré says, "I am in too. You need me and I want the immortality. Not really keen on becoming a vampire but as I am dating one now, immortality will ease a worry for me." My eyes widen and move to Malachi, sitting next to Memré with a big grin on his face. Memré continues, "I will need to visit my son but, not very often. He likes his independence. I will find some more security people to hire to cover my position in the foundation and we will work on bringing Olympus into the modern era."

"Excellent!"

Ajah says, "Ryna is still in mourning and she isn't ready for people right now, but she knew what you would be asking. She and I are in."

"I am so sorry, we all miss Seamus and feel his absence. Let her know she is welcome to take as long as she needs. The two of you are excused from the coronation if you don't feel up to going. If you do, please make sure I know very soon, so I can get dresses for you both."

We go around the table; Steve, John, Benny and Rico are all in. Brad looks around the table with sad eyes, "I can't do it. My girl. She… I have only just convinced her that it doesn't matter that we are different species when we shift. I need to stay here and I don't think she would ever forgive me if I became immortal."

I nod, "Brad, that is fine. I understand. I want each of you to do what is best for you and your family. Immortality is not all it is cracked up to be. It is hard and a lot to accept. That is why I wanted to have this meeting, I needed for you all to be able to make the decision knowing as much as possible. That said, I think we have covered everything, unless there are any questions?"

Owen asks, "Will my cell phone work on Olympus or will I need to come here to call my mom?"

I frown, "Owen, I have no idea. I will ask my parents, they might know. Or, we will find out together when we go."

Memré waves at me, "How is the immortality thing going to happen? Are you going to expect us to worship you or something? I don't know that I could do that with a straight face."

"Ha! No. I will not. Worship who you please. I believe that I can just bless you, but I didn't really get details from my mom when we were talking about the coronation. We will get it done this week—" I watch as a rather large spider lowers itself onto the table about midway down it. John raises his hand in preparation to smash it and I shout, "No! John! Do not touch the spider!"

John looks at me in surprise, I have never shouted at any of them. Before I can say anything the spider glows, a white light emanating from it and a woman in a black shimmery dress appears.

John's eyes widen, flustered he says, "I, I am so sorry. I didn't know. May I help you down?" He stands, knocking his chair over behind him as he does, but ignoring it in favor of offering a hand to the woman.

She smiles sweetly at him and takes his hand, swinging her legs down off the table and allowing him to aid her. Once she is standing he offers her his chair. She accepts his offer and he sets it upright behind her, pushing it in as she seats herself. I take this time to study her. She is small, thin with a slim body. The sheath type dress she wears hangs well on her slight frame. Her hair is dark and her eyes are darker, while her skin is pale. Now she is seated she turns to me, "I presume you are Fate?"

"I am. I am very happy to meet you Arachne. I confess, I didn't expect to see you so soon."

Nineteen

Arachne smiles widely, "It isn't everyday one gets to create a dress for the coronation of the new queen of the gods. I think it is fair to say that it hasn't happened in my lifetime and I have lived a very long time. There will be no other dress maker that will be able to make that claim. My fame will expand and I will provide my goddess with further prestige."

"You do Athena proud. I would ask though, is it possible that you can create dresses for the ladies of my court as well, if that is not too much? I do not want to pressure you at all."

Her eyes sparkle, "I would love to! The men's clothing would be no problem if you would permit me?"

"I would love that. You are amazing. Are you sure it isn't too much? I don't want to overburden you."

Malachi clears his throat, "I'll need mine to be a kilt.

When I dress for an occasion I wear kilts. I may not wear them daily, but I make sure to wear them for occasions."

Arachne nods, "That is not a problem." She looks back at me, "My only condition is that when the coronation and ball are done, you allow me and my girls to take the garments away for preservation and display. You will be welcome to them at any time, should you wish to wear them again. I have a museum of sorts and these will be a focal point for the tour."

"Oh! Yes! Of course! Do you need to measure us? I don't know anything about this process, having been just a regular witch until recently. A lot of what has come to pass has been well out of the realm of expected for me. I am happy to let you have the lead in this."

Arachne almost seems to swell in size as her grin takes over most of her face, she whispers, "Would you grant me free reign with the design? Are you saying that?"

"Yes, yes I would. To be honest, I needed Natasha here to learn how to dress myself for day to day occasions. My only request is that they do not constrict movement. There are… concerns about certain factions misbehaving and we may need to be more active than one usually would at a coronation."

Her eyes sparkle as she claps her hands in front of her, "I can hide weapons in the dresses? Oh! You are too gracious! Yes! Everyone will have apparel to make the heavens weep with the beauty of them. My girls will be here momentarily, we will measure you all thoroughly. We will return for a fitting before the coronation, when we will show you where all the weapons are hidden, and then we will go with you to the coronation to make sure everything is perfect." She claps her hands together twice and twelve women appear in a row behind her. "We need measurements for all of them. Thorough measurements, the queen has given me carte blanche with the design." The women's mouths drop briefly before they all grin and move around the room to start measuring people. Everyone is tugged from their chairs and very thoroughly measured. There are some startled yelps throughout the room as the ladies work. Arachne comes to me and says, "I will be doing the measurements for your highness."

"Oh, thank you." I say as I stand, "You don't need to call me your highness. You can call me Fate. One of the women is not in here, there was a death in our family and she was particularly close to them."

"As you wish, Fate. Can someone escort one of the women to this one for measurements? Please hold out your arms for me." She begins work and a small notepad flutters around with a pencil, and writes down my measurements as she goes. "You have given me such a gift, allowing me to create the dress as I please. It is so rare that anyone is willing to do that—" She stops and tips her head to one side as though listening to a voice only she can hear. "Oh yes! Indeed. As I was saying, it is so rare that anyone is willing to allow the designer free reign in this way. I am so honored to do so, especially with such a momentous occasion. You will be regal and dangerous, and you will outshine every queen that has ever been coronated, as you should since you are to be a queen of gods. I must measure your head now, I will need to stand in the chair to measure it properly."

"Here, take my hand to steady you as you get up there. But why my head? Is part of the dress going to be there?"

She giggles, "No, Hephaestus is creating your crowns. He needs the measurements to make sure they are fitted to you and no other. He was very vehement about that. I don't think he likes Apollo very much."

"Oh, is he making noise about becoming king?"

"He is. He wants to be the king of all but do nothing. He has grown large in recent times, his excesses are known far and wide. His rule would be a tragedy and I would not create for him."

"Oh my, you feel that strongly about it?"

"I do, he is not a person," she stops and looks me in the eye, "that I would ever be in a room with alone. I advise you and yours adopt the same policy."

"I see. Well, things are going to change," I say as I help her down from the chair, "I know it will be rough for a time but I think it is long overdue. We are going to put a stop to gods running amok and taking as they please."

Arachne lays a hand on my arm, "I think you will do very good things. Please be cautious as you do these things. Many of the gods are petty, selfish creatures with no concern for the damage they do. They will try to end your reign before it begins."

I press my lips together and nod. "I know. I will be

careful. Thank you, for the dress and for the advice. You and your work are appreciated."

"Thank you. I will take my leave now, we all have much work to do and a short time in which to do it. I will see you in a few days for the fitting."

I step back as she shimmers into nothing, I look around to see all the women that came to measure everyone are disappearing in the same manner.

"Well, thanks everyone. How fortunate that they came right then, while we were all still in the same room. Natasha, could you and Billy stay for a little longer. I have a gift for you."

Memré pats Natasha's shoulder on her way past, she knows what I have planned. She nods at me as she heads off to the kitchen, Malachi close behind. She looks happier and more at ease than I have ever seen her, it gives me joy to see it. I wait as everyone leaves, I think Ajah may not have stayed after she escorted one of the women back from measuring Ryna.

The room empties of everyone but us and the guys. "Natasha, I know how hard it has been for you, not being able to see Grams. So I talked with my parents and arranged for you to be able to see her. We can go right now, if you are ready."

Her eyes go round, "Yes! Let's go now! Oh good night I miss her so much! How do we go? Where is she? Is she here?"

"She is in Summerland, which is connected to the Underworld. Everyone clasp hands and don't let go. I don't know what happens if you let go in between places but I have to guess it is nothing good."

***

Fate

***

We arrive in our usual place, Cerberus runs out to greet us.

Hello! It's been so long! Hades said you would be bringing her very soon, I let him know you are here.

"Thank you Cerberus," I tell him as I scratch all his heads, "Will you be escorting us in today?"

Of course. It is my duty. And I enjoy it. You all are my favorites. Especially Charles and Devon, I love playing fetch with them. Makes my day. Will the new ones be playing too?"

"You know, I think some training for everyone sounds like a great idea. We can leave Natasha to talk with Griselda. She won't need us at all. Besides, Julian hasn't had the opportunity to train with you and neither has Billy. I would bet mom wants to show me some new to me dirty tricks too. With the coronation coming up, we should all be on our toes."

Two of Cerberus's heads lift up to grin at the guys while the third remains in my hands to be scratched. Charles and Devon groan, Julian chuckles.

Billy asks, "Why are you laughing?"

Julian grins, "Because I'm going to give him a run if he wants to catch me."

Billy laughs but Charles says, "Think you're faster than a vampire?"

Julian's grin grows, "I know I am, old man. You two aren't the first vampires I have ever annoyed."

Charles lifts an eyebrow, "I should be surprised if we were."

Cerberus chuffs at me and we lead everyone in to find my parents.

We find them in their office, after greetings and hugs I ask them if today is a good day for training, since we are here and have a couple extras for Cerberus to chase.

Hades says, "Yes. Please. We have a set of teens that have been overly energetic lately. They are going in with him because they need the run. Darling, why don't you go ahead with them, I know you want to spend time teaching Fate all the techniques you have learned. I will take Natasha to Griselda, who has been waiting for hours."

Persephone nods and gives my father a lingering kiss, we all immediately decide to wait in the hall. Long minutes later my mother and father come out of the office, only slightly disheveled.

My mother walks next to me as we head for the training area. I notice Cerberus has ditched us to go collect his teenagers. Mom asks me, "How did the fitting go?"

"It went well. I didn't know Hephaestus would be making me a crown. I thought I would just be wearing whatever Zeus had worn."

"Oh no. We can't have that. Zeus was a pompous jackass that walked around with a literal glow around his head so people would know he was king. It looked ridiculous. You will have a few crowns, Hephaestus insisted it be so and I don't know that he would take no for an answer. I think he is just happy to be making things that aren't weapons being used by a god with no honor. When he approached me he told me that he had known for a long time how corrupt Zeus is, he just didn't think anyone would believe him."

We reach the training area to find Cerberus and his teens lined up at the entrance to the run. Grinning.

Devon groans, "Could you pop in our suits? I am not dressed for this."

I laugh, "Would you like a suit as well, Julian? Billy?"

Billy looks at the dogs, all of them chewing on something that is making them drool excessively. "Yes, please."

Julian laughs, "Nah. I won't be wearing any clothes for this."

I call in three suits, handing them to all the guys except Julian who has stripped off his shirt but as his hands go to his pants his eyes flick over to my mother who smiles and turns her back to him. He sheds his pants and shoes, then quickly changes. His glorious wolf is near the size of Cerberus, bigger even than most of the teens. I step over to him, "Can I pet you?"

He huffs a little noise that sounds like a laugh as he nods. I thread my fingers through his fur, feeling the wire-y outer coat and the down-soft undercoat. I wrap my arms around him and lay my face against the side of his, my fingers wriggling, scratching their way through his fur. He tips his head downward to push me a little closer and I laugh as I release him. "All right, have fun storming the castle guys!"

Mom and I watch as they all walk toward the entrance. Cerberus and his children watch too, with much shifting and anticipation. They wait a full thirty seconds after everyone disappears into the maze before Cerberus lets out a howl and they all take off after them.

Mom laughs, "Your father loves this game. It is the highlight of his year so far."

Hades walks up from behind me over to my mother's side as he says, "I do love seeing them covered in drool. They hate it so much. I am going to go up high and watch, you two have fun. Natasha and Griselda were both crying and hugging when I left. I told her that Griselda could guide her over here when they are done."

"Thanks. Natasha really needed this. I haven't thought to ask with all the queen stuff going on, but where did you bury Trust and Kindness?"

My father tips his head to one side, "Why would I bury them? They are alive and healing with their mothers. I'll be sending them to Olympus as soon as they are back at full power."

He disappears and my mom says, "Come over here. There is a benefit that most gods don't know about to being one of Zeus's heirs. He had lightening as a naturally occurring weapon. Most of his heirs do as well. Now, this means that any of his other heirs could and possibly have, figured this out. So they may have access to lightening as well. Most have not, and I know Apollo would have tried it on me if he had, because I anger him as often as I can."

I followed with my mouth hanging open, "Mom, what do you mean? You anger him as often as you can? Why?"

She lifts one shoulder in a shrug and tells me, "He is an egotistical jackass with shredded paper bits for brains. It delights me to frustrate him into silence and it would be fantastic if he got mad enough to do something about it."

"Erm, well, ok."

"Anyway, the lightening. Energy like that doesn't just hang out in any one place. It is constantly running through your veins. Your job is to call it to your hand. You might have to whisper to it at first, but once the path is created for release, it will come to your will faster each time. I started out picturing something like an energy field just under my skin. Then I pictured an opening in my hand for it to form a bolt. After that finally worked, I threw it like a spear. You try it. We have time, breathe and focus."

I close my eyes and try to picture the energy current under my skin but I hear claws tapping on the floor. I open my eyes and look to the maze to see Charles and Devon being carried over by Cerberus and one of his children. They are dripping wet so I call in a fresh stack of towels as they are gently deposited in front of us.

Cerberus throws the thought, *Favorites!* at us as he and his child turn to run back into the maze. Charles gets his face cleaned off, "How wonderful. We are the dog's favorite chew toys."

My mother was the one that broke my control with her giggle. I could have held back from laughing until I heard that. It was all over the minute she giggled, we were both lost in laughter after that. We were still laughing as Cerberus triumphantly came back with Julian dangling from his mouth. His fur soaked with drool but a wolfish grin on his face. Behind him another of Cerberus' children carries Billy. They deposit them near to the guys and turn around, trotting off into the maze to wait for the return of their playmates.

Julian stretches a bit, winks at me and then shakes his entire body. Furry drool goes flying everywhere. Persephone and I collapse in laughter as Julian takes off for the maze with the three vampires hot on his heels. We calm ourselves shortly after all of them enter the maze again. Standing, I dust myself off. A few deep breaths and I close my eyes, working on seeing the energy flowing through my body. I am feeling nothing so far and I remember that she said I might have to whisper to it the first time. I feel awkward as hell but I start whispering as quietly as I can, "Come on, I know you're in there. Work with me." I feel just the slightest stirring of something. Something is listening so I keep talking, "Come, follow the path I made for you. We will practice making things explode. You want to run and play, don't you? Give me a chance. I will prove myself worthy. I promise I won't use you to hurt innocents. Only ever after I have been attacked. But now, we need to practice in case things go really wrong. Help me, us." My heartfelt plea did something as I feel an energy rushing to my hand, I open my eyes to see a long bolt of lightening form. I whisper thank you as I swing my arm up and back, I aim for a target in the middle as best I can and fling my arm forward, releasing the bolt at nearly the full extension of my arm. It hits a target two spaces to the right of where I intended.

My mother claps and whoops in celebration, "You did it! You did it on your first real try! I am so proud of you!" She sweeps me up into a hug and dances around a bit before releasing me and saying, "Now do it again. Aim better, I know you weren't aiming for that one. You can do this!"

I practice throwing lightening until I think my arms will fall off. It isn't enough that I get it right with one hand, nope. I have to be ambidextrous with this stuff. All of the guys are brought out by Cerberus and his crew multiple times, though Julian avoids them the most. By the time Natasha and Griselda come to find us the guys are all thoroughly tired of the game and laying down on the floor not far from us. I hit the target again just as they enter. I am relieved to see them, I think my mother would not have let me quit until they were done, however long it took.

Griselda gives me a hug and tells the guys that they smell. My father comes walking out of the maze with Cerberus, his pups having vanished to report in to their mothers. Billy reaches for Natasha and she steps back out of reach, "No sir. Grams was absolutely right. You stink. Shower, then you can touch me."

He chuckles weakly and drops his hand. Persephone walks over to join Hades, and she says, "You all did very well today. Hermes might be able to catch you if he tried. Staying out of the clutches of the other gods will be key to keeping you alive. Most of them will not be able to do what Fate can do and with the exception of a few, they do not practice fighting. They will be slower but they will also be angry and playing for keeps. The more of you they get rid of the weaker her defense. You are more valuable to her alive than dead, when you die you cannot protect her. Yes, she is a goddess and more powerful than any of you but math works the same no matter who you are and there are more of them."

Hades looks darkly at them, "I will be most displeased if she is captured or if any of you get yourselves killed. However, it still isn't me you should worry about. She," he points at my mother, "will be irate and less than reason-able." My mother slants him a look and he slips an arm around her, "I wouldn't have you any other way my love, but it is bad news for them."

The guys are looking very serious at this point, heaving themselves to their feet. Devon says, "We understand. We won't let you down."

My mom says, "See that you do not."

I walk over and hug my parents, "I have to get everyone back home, so they can shower. That smell really is wretched." They laugh as they hug me and I groan as I put my arms back down. Somehow I thought being a goddess meant the end of muscle aches, only so far it has meant that my challenges are that much tougher. Stepping over to the guys I see that Julian has shifted while I was hugging my parents and thrown on his pants. We all take hands, in some cases reluctantly, and I pop us back home.

Twenty

FATE

Coronation day has arrived and I have giant eagle sized butterflies cavorting in my stomach. Arachne is here to help us into our dresses and make any last minute adjustments. My dress is too much, I don't know if I can pull it off. It is this whisper soft material against my skin with a silken overlay in a deep jewel-tone red, over that is a black lace that could be hung spider's webbing it is so delicate. Tiny rubies sparkle and glitter, dotting the lace like tiny red stars. The bodice is a deep vee and the body of the dress looks like it is a mermaid style but Arachne showed me the elastic on the inside that create the pleats on the back of the dress to make it look like that. The train is attached with tiny magnets and will detach if pulled on. That could be embarrassing for me if I catch it on something or a life-saver if we have to fight and someone tries to drag me back with it. She also spends time showing each of us again where the weapons are hidden in our clothing. I have two knives in my bodice, small but I bet they would do the trick in a pinch.

All in all, the dress is stunning and I have never worn anything have so lovely. Natasha's dress is a deep emerald green, while Ajah and Ryna wear gold and black. Memré got this dark blue dress that sets her skin off perfectly and might have made her eyes leak a little when she saw herself in the mirror. My loves all have red accents for their suits and Malachi has dark blue accents. The rest of my bodyguards are accented with a lighter shade of red.

Maria made sure all the vampires were very well fed, she pushed bags of blood on each of them and that was before the food. She brought out enough food to feed an army. Of starving wolves. I don't know when she started cooking but wow. We all ate very well. Or, well, they did. I haven't been able to eat much because I was more than a little concerned that I might throw up.

Persephone pops into the room as Arachne and two of her people are finishing the arrangement inspection of my dress. I haven't done anything with my hair yet and mom looks hard at my hair piled high on my head to keep it out of the way. "Fate, would you mind it terribly if I brought some people for your hair? The high pile doesn't really say love and fear me the way the dress does."

I laugh, "Yes. Please. I need the help. Everyone else is

ready already, I just didn't know what to do with my hair. Or my makeup."

Mom nods, "Perfect. I have just the people." She snaps her fingers and two elvish looking men appear, they look from my mother to me and back again with raised eyebrows. She lowers hers and they look back at me with friendlier expressions. Sort of.

They are both pale but one is wearing green while the other is wearing brown. The green clad one asks, "Is that style on purpose?"

"Oh no! This was just to get it out of the way while Arachne worked her part of the magic."

"Good. Good. I was concerned." He looks back at my mother, "Norse type braids? With the lower half left to drape down her back?"

She nods, "That should be just the look she needs."

The brown clad one has been studying me this whole time and he finally speaks, "I think red and black, smoky eye. Do you have any objection to that?"

"I do not. I may be fighting later, so maybe we can seal this stuff on my face magically to stay until I wash it?"

"Oh yes, it wouldn't do for your eye makeup to run down your face mid-coronation."

A chair appears behind me and I sit down very carefully, Arachne taking the faux train off first. I get myself positioned comfortably in the chair and they go to work. Mr. Green starts with the braids, while Mr. Brown starts with using a cotton ball to smooth a liquid over my face. Or maybe he is cleaning it, who knows? They work on me and the whole thing just feels so nice, I begin to drift. My thoughts turn to the time right after my husband died. I thought for sure that my life was over now that the only person that ever really loved me had died.

I never imagined that I could have a huge family of people that love me, the people I grew up thinking were my family hated me. And now that I have spoken to them in the afterlife, well, I know that they were forced into adopting me and really resented me for it. I know it had nothing to do with me, but I suffered for it just the same.

To have parents that love me the way that Persephone and Hades do, is my wildest dreams come true. They are stern, and will push me to my very limits with training but at the same time would think to do things like hiring Arachne for my dress and Hephaestus to create a crown or two for me and bring someone to do my makeup and my hair. Or lead a charge to rescue me from their own family.

All that and three mates. Three! All gorgeous in their own right while being absolutely devoted to me. I couldn't have pictured a life like this no matter what glasses I wore back then. All I have to do is make it through being crowned and I will actually get to live my fairytale. Hopefully Apollo won't challenge but if he does then I will choose a champion. And if things devolve into a whole battle, well, we will burn that bridge when we get to it. I just have to ensure my family survives. Oh! I know! I will set shields on every one of them. I go ahead and send out the magic to shield my family. They won't entirely stop a god, obviously, but it may slow them down enough for my family to get away or for me to blast the shit out of them with my lightening.

I feel a tap on my shoulder and open my eyes. Mr. Brown is looking into my eyes, saying "I need your eyes open for the mascara." I hold very still as he does that, I do not want to be stabbed in the eye. He finishes saying, "There! You are more lovely even than before. Go forth and be crowned."

I feel my cheeks heat, "Thank you. I appreciate all your work." I turn to look for Mr. Green, "and yours as well, I know my hair is set beautifully now."

He smiles with real pleasure and I notice his teeth are quite pointed as he tells me, "We worked spells so that no one will be able to grab you by the hair, it will simply slip from their hands, no matter where they try to grab it. With the possibility of a battle, we thought it best. The spell will wear off sometime tomorrow."

"Thank you! You are both wonderful, I would not have thought of that."

Mr. Brown says, "It is our duty to think of these things. Here is our card, should you need our services in the future, all you will need to do is read the words out loud."

I accept the card and they disappear. My mother steps forward, "You look beautiful and you charmed Lith and Solm. They are notoriously haughty and quite rude on the best of occasions. They have good reason, but still. They were nice to you the entire time!"

"What? Why? Is there something I should know for future keeping me from saying something dumb?"

My mother's face falls, "Yes, I suppose there is. They are outcast from their kind. They were banished for being a couple. Now, many of those that were part of banishing them, that keep them banished, beg to use their services. They pose as regular human artists that work for the stars. Half their time is spent telling their relatives to go away."

"That is awful. So don't mention their family ever and don't be shitty. Got it. I think I can manage that one. I guess now it's time to head for Olympus. How are we going to get there?"

"I will take you all this first time. Once you know where it is, you will be able to pop back and forth as you please. Everyone gather in and hold hands." I watch as Arachne and her people disappear, she is holding the train to my dress still so I know she has gone to Olympus. Natasha and Memré step up next to me and as I take their hands for this momentous trip, it somehow feels like this is how it should happen. My best friends at my side as I go to claim my crown.

I expected Olympus to be more… showy? It is still all old pillars, stone floors, and chairs made of rocks. Of course we are still outside, that may have something to do with it. My mother sees my face and tells me, "The decor inside has not changed any more than this, though there are better chairs and couches inside. Once the coronation is over, you may shape it to your liking."

I nod as those eagle-sized butterflies start cavorting in my belly again. The walkway is short and in no time we are in the building. The inside is all marble, in remarkable condition. It is expansive, the rooms would echo if they were not open to the breezes. We reach a smaller room and mom tells me, "We are behind the throne room, this is where you will wait until it is time for the ceremony. Hera has agreed to be the one to crown you. She is really looking forward to leaving this place. Her quarters are emptied of her belongings. She left Zeus' room untouched. She told me that she would never clean up after him again. You can deal with that later, but you may want to check his room for little objects of power or writings that would be of use to you. For now, your father is out there with Aries, Athena, and Hera. They are all playing the part of gracious hosts until it is time for the ceremony. We have hope that it will go without challenge. Apollo was drinking heavily with Dionysus last we saw. He may be intentionally occupying Apollo but we will never know. I do advise that you do not drink anything he brings to the party. That goes for all of you."

We all nod our agreement. I see a curtain and move to peek out. The throne lays before me, I see Poseidon arriving and greeting my father with a hearty hug that is reciprocated. Hera is speaking to a couple of women, they are all laughing as one holds her thumb and forefinger an inch apart in demonstration. There are men I haven't met having an animated conversation with Aries and

Aphrodite. I see the one I think is Hephaestus taking his ease on a cushioned chair off to one side.

Hera claps her hands and says, "It is time!" I step back, away from the curtains.

My mother puts an arm around my shoulders. "You are going to do great. Come stand over here while I get everyone lined up." She guides me to the back of the room where Arachne waits with my train. She quickly fastens it to my dress as mother lines everyone up, giving them swift directions on where to stand once they are out there. She makes it back to me and says, "You will stay close to the throne, come up from the left side and meet Hera in front of it. She will speak, crown you, and then you will sit on the throne. Deep breath, you were born for this my daughter."

As she finishes so does Hera and the line ahead of me begins to move out through the curtains. A lifetime or three seconds later I am stepping through the curtain and onto a dias to the left of the throne. Hera waits for me and I walk with measured steps to her, stopping within arms reach.

She smiles and nods her head slightly then we turn to the crowd as she says, "And here is Fate, daughter of Persephone and Hades, a true queen to usher in a new era for us all. Who supports her rule?"

I watch the crowd as my father and mother both say I do. Aries, says "I support her rule." He looks darkly at some of the others. Aphrodite, Poseidon, Athena, and Hekate all throw in their I do's as well.

"Are there any who would challenge her right to rule?"

A drunken man in the back of the room stands, falls and farts, then climbs heavily back up with the support of a column. He slurs, "I would, I wan challenge. Is my riii-ightful throne." Then he falls to the floor unconscious. I look around and then whisper, "Do we have to wait till he wakes up?"

"No dear. Watch this." Hera speaks to the crowd again, "Challenger, you must come and present yourself before the throne at once or your challenge is voided as the ravings of a man that has had too much drink. I will give you to the count of five. One…Two…Three…Four… Five."

He begins to snore loudly in the back, two men lift his feet and drag him from the room.

Hera shrugs and tells the crowd, "I suppose he didn't want it all that bad then. As there are no other chal-lengers," she lifts a gorgeous crown of burnished dark gold vine work with rubies set in each of the peaks and turns back to me, "I, Hera, Queen of the Gods do now bestow upon you the title of Queen of the Gods. May you rule in peace, with justice and equality." She sets the crown upon my head and whispers, "Go sit in the chair to seal the deal." I take the two steps and turn, my train moving along almost like it has help. I sit down on the throne and the room erupts in cheers. I set my face into a smile, even as my heart is beating like wild birds trying to escape a cage. Queen. I am queen of the gods. I can't believe it.

The other gods form a loose sort of line and each

greets me, wishing me well. Some indicate they would wish to speak to me privately and I put them off as politely as I can. Dionysus appears before me with a roguish smile, "Care for a drink my queen?"

I smile, "Thank you but no. I think I must keep my head for the foreseeable future. And I think we have seen what strong drink will do to the unwary."

He laughs loudly, "Oh! You will do just fine. Apollo would make a worse ruler than Zeus ever was and the rare times he is honest with himself, he knows that. You do your thing, I will keep Apollo drunk with me for the next few hundred years while you change our world. It'll be better that way." With his peace said, Dionysus winks at me a strides off into the crowd. I think if he ever became ambitious, he would be a force to be reckoned with.

Hours later the line of gods finally ends and my mother moves to the front of the dias, "Everyone, let us move to the ballroom for refreshments and dancing."

Twenty-One

   I am last to enter the ball room, it is a strange feeling to know all eyes are on me and not for reasons of egg on my face. Arachne removed the train as we walked the hall. She congratulated me on a relatively peaceful transfer of power while warning me that I should still be wary. Devon, Charles, and Julian are my escorts as I enter. My mother whispers to me, "No one can dance until you do, that is the signal for things to loosen up a little."

   Devon smiles and asks, "May I have this dance?"

   I feel the smile spread across my face, I have never been asked to dance before. "Yes, you may good sir." He whisks me away in his arms and somehow it doesn't seem to matter that I have never danced in this life, all the ones before did and the knowledge seems to live in me somewhere. Or maybe I just feel like I am on cloud nine dancing with my Devon.

We are joined on the floor by others though a space is left around us. Devon says, "You were always my queen and now you are a literal queen. Are you happy love?"

I think about it for a moment. With all the events of recent weeks, the deaths; am I happy? My heart feels light and overflowing with joy, even though there is some sorrow mixed in, "You know, I am. I am really happy in a way that I never thought to be. Thank you Devon, I am so glad you walked into my library that day. You started me on the strangest of paths but I got to have you beside me. I love you."

"And I love you. I never expected to see you there when I walked in that day but I regret nothing. You are—"

We stop and I see Charles has tapped Devon's shoulder, "May I cut in?"

Devon takes my face in his hands and presses a soft kiss to my lips before he nods to Charles. He walks off with a lightness in his step that I haven't seen in this lifetime. Charles takes me in his arms as the music changes and we dance to a slower, more sensual song. He holds me close as he says, "I want to apologize for kidnapping you but I'm not sorry. Had I not taken you that day, you would never have known me and your goddess side could not have activated. I do apologize for all the murder. That was really not well done on my part. I hope you will forgive me anyway."

"Oh Charles, I forgive you. I will say that other than biting and turning me without permission you were a good host. I don't know that we had any choice in whether or not we somehow found each other. Either way, I am glad you forced the issue and that I had the courage to stand my ground on making you take me home."

He laughs and then we stop dancing once again, I see Julian standing next to us. Charles drawls, "Hello Juli, can I help you?"

Julian grins, a little wolfish even in his human form, "May I cut in?" he asks as the music changes. Charles nods but grabs me and pulls me close to give me a kiss that could have scorched the tiles beneath us before he gently releases me into Julian's arms.

I shake my head to clear it after that kiss, Julian whispers, "Your flames are showing."

My cheeks light up with a blush as I work to calm them, but he takes me in his arms and we start dancing as he says, "Don't put them out, they are fascinating. Not as fascinating as the light show you put on when you cum, but fascinating none the less."

I laugh, "You say the sweetest things Julian. I'm sorry we haven't had much opportunity to get to know each other."

He shrugs, "We have forever. I can be patient knowing that you are mine. And since meeting you I have stepped into this amazing life that has far eclipsed anything I could have hoped or dreamed."

"Oh Julian, I don't know what to say. I'm not sure I deserve you."

"I can assure you, whether or not you are deserving has

never been a question in my mind. You are amazing even when you can't see it."

Our dance ends and he guides me from the floor to a small, informal throne type chair. Devon and Charles are waiting there for me with refreshments. They have set up a small table near the throne. I sit and they move the table in front of me with Devon explaining, "We brought this food, it is not from the tables across the room which have been adulterated with various substances." He looks across the room, "I get the impression that a lot of them wanted to eat the adulterated items? So maybe it isn't bad things but probably still better that you don't partake."

I nod as I dig in to the food, I find that I am hungry now. I suppose all that anxiety makes for a hearty appetite once the cause of the anxiety is gone. My mother steps up to the dias, "Your highness can go or stay as she pleases, she has done her duty in regards to the coronation." She smiles widely at me, "I am so proud of you daughter. Go, have a good night. The morning will bring plenty that needs your attention."

"Thank you mom, I don't know what I would do without you and dad." She wipes away a tear as she turns to go back to my father. I look around at my guys, "How do you feel about getting out of here?"

Charles says, "We thought you'd never ask."

I stand and take Devon's arm, Julian rushes up to take my other. Charles follows behind saying, "I have always loved the view from here."

Mercy of the Vampire King

What kind of fool would beg mercy from a vampire, even if he is a king?

Valdís

I have one hope to keep my title, lands, and the people we are supposed to take care of out of the hands of my mother and sister. I must beg the vampire kings to grant me aid and just hope they aren't hungry as people that annoy them have a way of disappearing. Arriving at the castle, I realize I am in way over my head when the scent of the king lights a fire in my soul that could get me killed.

Knox

King of a land that is nothing more than a myth to the rest of the world, I just want my time in charge to pass quickly. Until she arrives, begging so sweetly. Her blood sings to mine and her attitude promises anything but the monotony of late. What seemed like nothing more than a family dispute over inheritance becomes more when they try to take all our lives.

War

My quest to save my people revealed worlds of treachery, and now the Outsiders are back. Once again, looking to take our country. The king may have mercy on my people but at what cost?

Mercy of the Vampire King *is the first in the completed Vampire Kings series. For fans of Geneva Lee or Katee Robert, this is a steamy, paranormal romance with a happily ever after at the end of the series.*

A Free Story for You!

Enjoyed A Vampire's Fate? Not ready to quit reading yet? If you sign up for my newsletter at

https://www.subscribepage.com/r4v6m2 , where you will receive Fated for Halloween, the origin story of Fate's Chronicles, right away as my thank you gift for choosing to hang out with me.

Or, how Fate's Chronicles began.
I like to think I was a happy Goddess, even when my mother was incredibly tiresome. All that changed when the Beast showed up on our doorstep. Escaping the confines of the house and the terrible way the Beast looks at me I find a dark stranger sunbathing naked in my field.

The violence within...
He is trying to kill me. I want to believe my mother

will protect me but my dark stranger feels safer than this home or my mother ever have. I have to make a choice soon, or my life will be ended before it has really begun.

Whoever I choose, my life will never be the same again.

Kore yelled toward the interior of the house from near the front door, "Mother, I'm off to my field, I feel a need to be outside with my thoughts. I'll return soon."

"Waaaaaiiiiitttt!!!"

Kore rolled her eyes, she knew she shouldn't have even hoped she could get away so easily she listens as her mother runs to intercept her before she leaves the house. As if she were going somewhere her mother couldn't find her. Or that was even off the property.

Huffing and puffing Demeter rounded the corner at full speed with her head tucked down. Kore could see that she would not be able to stop in time as she hadn't yet realized she was in the entryway. Kore neatly stepped to the left before her mother could plow into her, leaving Demeter to hit the wall in front of her. It didn't seem to faze her though it did stop her. She turned around searching until her eyes light upon her most coveted child, Kore. For her part Kore waited patiently for her mother to gather her wits and try to force her to stay in the house under her stifling presence. Demeter draws in, uncomfortably close to her daughter, placing a hand on her shoulder and speaking directly into her face, "Oh sweet girl, why would you want to go out there? It's all bugs and muggy heat. You should stay here in the house where it is lovely and cool. What if some man crosses your path? He could do terrible things to your reputation!"

Kore's eyes move toward the ceiling of their own volition, "Mother, please. What do I care if some man hinges my reputation on whether or not I have been in the company of other men? Because I have been in the company of men, Beltane is my holiday. My favorite time of the year and I take at least one lover every year at the fires. My reputation is that I am the Goddess of Spring and New Beginnings, not some spinster. I am grown mother. I live here simply to humor you. I will not become a prisoner of your house."

Demeter grabbed her heart with one hand and the wall with the other, "My heart, oh my heart, why don't you just rip it out already? My own daughter treats me like this! No Goddess of the Harvest and Seasons ever had a daughter so ungrateful!"

Foot tapping Kore says, "I am going mother. Are you quite finished?"

Peering up through her lashes to see that Kore isn't falling for it at all Demeter straightened up, having decided to take a different tack, "Fine. You don't care about your mother, the least you could is take your maidens with you. You'll want to be married one day and you'll thank me then. Take the maidens if you must go."

"Fine. If that will stop your harping, tell them to come. Now will you go back to whatever it was that you were doing?"

Demeter bellowed into the house, "Girls! Come escort my daughter!" Turning back to Kore she says, "No, I can't go back to what I was doing as now I must lay down, sick with worry that you might be ravished while you wander like a thoughtless child."

"You know, I have always loved a good ravishing, you probably shouldn't worry about that mother."

"Impudent child!"

"I am over a century old mother, childhood is long gone."

The maidens Demeter summoned arrived and Kore opened the door, they filed out with her following the last one out the door. Kore left the door standing open because she knew it would irritate her mother. The women followed the path through the woods surrounding the house, emerging out into a bright field that extends as far as the eye can see. Kore looks at the maidens, "Let's all lay down in this soft grass to enjoy the rays of this glorious sun." The maidens, her mother's little spies, agreed and picked a spot fluffy with clover. Kore laid down with them, waited for them to grow comfortable and with a wave of her hand sent them all to sleep.

Rising from her spot in the clover Kore shook her head and started walking out into her field. The combination of rolling hills, wild flower filled meadow and bright sunny day did much to improve her dark mood. As she walked she realized there was a dark hole ahead of her that should not be there and decided to investigate. Striding through the field she drew near the cave and was only a few feet away she noticed the body laid bare for all to see in her field.

There, laying in the grass was a gorgeous man. His clothing lay in a pile next to him but they were just clothes and not near so interesting as the hard planes of him. His eyes were closed so Kore let hers roam freely over all that gorgeous exposed flesh. His hair was dark and appeared long, how long she couldn't tell. His face, all strong angles and smooth beard with long lashes that lay against his cheeks, those looked soft as down. His shoulders broad, just the right kind for throwing a body over if he were interested in taking her off to ravish. The very thought caused a flood of moisture in her core. Those well formed shoulders led to an eight pack that looked like a ladder straight to the vee over the patch of dark curls where his shaft rested. It was soft at the moment but still an impressive size and Kore had seen enough members to be a fair judge. His legs were thick and powerful looking, as were his arms. Over all he was very well proportioned and Kore wouldn't mind a more prolonged and active visit with him.

"If you've had your eyeful, why not have a lie down in this gorgeous sun?"

"Oh! I didn't realize you were awake. My apologies, I should have called out. Though you are in my field."

"I don't mind. Have your fill of looking, but the sun really is very nice. You might give sunbathing a go. I have it on very good authority that today will continue to be a very nice day. Go ahead, I won't peek and I can assure you I will not ravish you."

Kore dropped her clothing during his little speech and is laying down when he finishes. She laughs, "Well, that is disappointing. I love a good ravishing." Turning her head she watched as he grimaces.

Lips still twisted and never opening his eyes he said, "You are probably completely inexperienced and vanilla is not my favorite flavor, nor am I interested in teaching anyone."

Kore's laughter rang thru the field, "What? Oh my, no." She rolled to her side and propped her head on her hand, "I hate to be the one to destroy your illusion of having been found by a fair maid with no experience to speak of, but I am not her. I am the Goddess of Spring and new beginnings, my whole season is about having as much sex as possible. Frankly, I am what hunts the hunters in the woods. Mother hates it, which is why she has taken to sending maidens out with me. But I just put them to sleep.

And Beltane! Beltane is my holy day, it infuriates mother that she cannot stop my attendance at the fires."

One of his eyes opens, "OH really?" She watched as his eye roamed her body.

"Yes, really. My time out is limited before mother comes hunting me and finds her maidens at the edge of the field. Care for a tryst in the sun before I must leave?"

His cock twitched when she said tryst, making her grin. Both his eyes are open now taking in her form and finally meeting her eyes, "Are you quite sure that you would want to tryst with one so mired in the Underworld as I?" He sits up, waving his hand at the cave and his appearance is darker, blue fire seeming to play at the tips of his hair. His dark eyes are soul deep, Kore could get lost in there. His darkness doesn't frighten her, no, it calls the darkness in her.

She noted the surprise on his face as she leans toward him and ever so gently touches her lips to his and whispers, "More than anything I have ever wanted in my entire long life. Your darkness feeds my starving soul."

Kore drew back, put enough space between them that she could see his eyes as she brought a hand up to his face, and caressed his cheek. His eyes drifted shut as he leaned in to the softness of her hand. She trailed her hand down the column of his neck and across his chest then traced the lines of his abs as his breath grew ragged. His hand shots out and grabbed hers before she could reach the goal that strained toward her wandering hand.

"Before we go any farther princess, beware that being

with me might taint your pretty little soul in a way those hunters and Beltane fire lovers cannot."

Kore laughed and dropped the control that kept the rest of her nature hidden from people like her mother. The meadow darkened though the day remained bright. Kore's pale blue eyes darkened to a color more indigo and her pale skin becomes bluish, her hair going from blond to white and seeming to float in its own breeze.

Hades had never seen anything so beautiful as Kore without her mask of innocence, he could live in her shadow if only he would be allowed to gaze upon her. Lucky for him it appeared that she wanted more than for him to live in her shadow.

Kore tugged her hand from his grip and used it to urge him to lie back down as she crawled over top him.

***

Hours later the two lie spent in the grass, Kore realizes the sun has nearly left the sky. "I must go back now, the maidens will be waking soon and I need to be there when they do." Sitting up she reached for her clothing and began dressing.

Hades also sat up, "I should probably go tend the Underworld, send some souls where they belong. Do you have a name other than princess?"

Giggling as she slipped her dress over her head she said, "Of course I do. My name is Kore. Do you have a name dark man of the Underworld?"

"I am Hades. You could say I am *the* dark man of the underworld. Will you come see me again?" He asks as he reached for her hand and used it to tug her closer before he wrapped his arms around her.

"I can't get away often. I would like to see you again. How will I get word to you when I can sneak away? Surely now that you know my name you know as well, Hades, the reputation of my mother in regard to me. The same as I know of your reputation as the dark lord of the Underworld, ruthless and evil as they come."

"That doesn't bother you?"

Snuggled into his chest she said, "No, not a bit. This has been the best afternoon I have spent in many years. Now, how will I contact you? I really must get going. They will wake when the sun touches the horizon."

Hades pulls a black feather from a pocket of his drape, "When you would have me pull out this feather and hold it in your hand. Bring it to your lips and blow on it. I will arrive here presently."

She took the feather from his hand and slipped it into a hidden pocket within her dress. A quick kiss pressed to his lips, Kore stood and took off running, yelling goodbye over her shoulder as she went. Looking toward the sun Hades saw that it is no more than an inch above the horizon.

Kore made it back to the maidens and lay down just a bare breath before they woke up. Pretending to wake up with them Kore stood and dusted the grass off her clothing,

"Let us go back to the house, mother will be worried. We have slept the afternoon away in the sun."

Fated for Halloween is only available by subscribing to my once monthly newsletter at:

https://www.subscribepage.com/r4v6m2

Epilogue

FATE

In the months since I was crowned nothing has slowed down. The Silseth family showed up at the house one day with a trailer full of books. Natasha was there with Billy and she cursed them soundly for trying to hoard those books while Billy laughed. Then she made them cart all the books to the doorway of the library, and had Owen stand there to hand books in to Brad who put them in stacks off to one side for cataloging.

She called me when they were finished and I popped down to restore their abilities in my full regalia. I informed them that there would be a school of sorts on Olympus very soon and the entire family would be expected to attend at least two semesters for the purpose of unifying the magical world. Clarinda is pissed but keeps her mouth shut.

The other families trickled in, they were all much more

receptive to everything. I think the Silseth family were vocal about their treatment. The Brooks family turned out to be really nice, some of them are coming to teach at the school as is Constantine Rosales. He is the last of his line but I have hope that perhaps he will find someone being in contact with so many of the magical community.

Natasha is thriving in the most amazing ways as she gets the foundation set up and works with the magical community. My father and mother have decided to let Griselda visit her on earth regularly since the training she should have had did not happen, and maybe a little because they just adore my friends.

Memré and Malachi have thrown themselves into the modernisation of Olympus, we have connected to the internet now. I don't know how they did it and I don't want to ask any questions because I feel certain that they bullied some people to make it so.

Brad has left, he is doing whatever the woman he loves asks and she wanted him to work with her father. I sent him with a very nice severance package and his retirement package. John, Owen, and Steve are having a magnificent time. They train with Cerberus every chance they get and are thrilled that they get to be immortal. Owen told me recently that his mother is so happy knowing that her son will be watching over the family long after she was gone. He said that she felt more peace knowing that than she had since his father died. I cried. It frightened Owen and he apologized profusely until I told him it was just so sweet and sad that his mom felt that way.

I found my sister, she is living with a man named Chad and they are both incredibly happy so I kept myself hidden. My sister was not very kind to me in a lot of ways, but I think now that maybe we were both victims of circumstance in a lot of ways. I blessed her home and then I left back to Olympus.

Trust and Kindness met me as I appeared, I was so thrilled to see them hale and hearty again. They stalk the halls and fields of Olympus now, with my protections on them as my power grew exponentially when I was crowned. I coaxed a small amount of lightening into them too, with the direction to protect them. I must say, watching Julian frolic with them gives me no end of amusement. My three loves have settled themselves into a routine of rotation for who gets to sleep in my bed. I love it, it is one less thing for me to worry about since they worked it out themselves.

Apollo is still making noise about being king and Dionysus has him drink to that every time or so Aries reports. He seems to have reformed his lying ways but he and Poseidon flirt outrageously every time they come to visit. Devon, Charles, and Julian do not appreciate it. I think that is the draw for Aries as he seems to be entirely wrapped around Aphrodite's little finger.

Prometheus is heading the school. He is brilliant and still wants to aid humanity, I want to channel that in the best way possible. And I want to let him live a happy life, free of Caucasion Eagles eating his liver daily. I have had to tell the bird shifters that come to the school not to change around him and no flying in. I hope he will heal one day but for now, this is the best I can do.

As for me, well, I am queen and it is good to be queen. My life has exploded into amazing in a way I could not have imagined less than a year ago. I have this amazing family that loves me and parents that would tear down the fabric of time itself to ensure my safety. I have three lovers that delight in my joy and the blessing of that is more than I ever expected.

My name is Fate, Goddess of the Blessed Death and the Blessed Beginning, Queen of the Gods.

Author's Note

I have truly loved taking this journey with Fate. Watching her grow and blossom into a role that I didn't even know she was going to have at the beginning of this series has been a ride I certainly did not expect.

Fate continually snatched plot bunnies from the ether and lobbed them into the story, creating no end of havoc on my side. The arc I started with for the series in book one was completely thrown out by the midpoint of book two. Queen of the Gods and killing Zeus? That was all Fate's idea. (She is really a lot pushier in person.)

However, while this is the final book in Fate's Chronicles, it is not the final book with a sassy heroine from me. If you haven't already met her, I would like to introduce you to Jasmine. Her life hasn't been the easiest and it is just ramping up to see exactly how much she can handle. You'll find an excerpt from her first book, Sin on a Dark Knight, in the pages following. I am working on her second book as I write this note, the pre-order link for it should be up in August 2021.

I am constantly working on the next book so check out the next page to find more of my work.

That said, I hope you loved this series as much as I did. It really helps me if you leave a review, so that would be great. But if you don't do reviews, that is cool too. Thank you for reading!

Rhiannon

Rhiannon writes steamy paranormal romance. She is an avid reader of many authors in a variety of genre though she tends more toward paranormal.

She has three former pound puppies that she dotes on and three daughters that she adores.

Rhiannon has lived in multiple states though she is currently residing in North Carolina. Wandering, witching, and reading with her puppies and husband are what she does when she isn't writing.

To learn about what is happening in Rhiannon's world and get loads of pupper cuteness, sign up for the by using the QR code below to visit my website.

Also by Rhiannon Futch

The Daughter of the Moon series-

<u>Selena Rose, Daughter of the Moon Book 1</u>

<u>Thorns of the Rose, Daughter of the Moon Book 2</u>

<u>Heart of the Rose, Daughter of the Moon Book 3</u>

The Fate's Chronicles series

<u>A Vampire's Fate</u>

<u>A Vampire's Treasure</u>

<u>A Vampire's Dream</u>

<u>A Vampire's Chase</u>

<u>A Vampire's Fight</u>

<u>Fated for Halloween -</u> only available via email signup

The Belancore Witches of North Carolina series

<u>Witchy Ever After</u>

<u>A Witchy New Year</u>

<u>My Witchy Valentine</u>

Sin series

<u>Sin on a Dark Knight</u>

<u>Sin on a Broken Heart</u>

<u>Sin on a Burning Heart</u>

Sin on a Vengeful Heart

The Vampire Kings Series

Mercy of the Vampire King

Shame of the Vampire King

Pursuit of the Vampire King

Prey of the Vampire King

Reign of the Vampire King

Coming Soon

Love and Vampires Series

Olivia's Fall

Olivia's Prison

Olivia's Flight

Olivia's Family

Warriors of the Old Gods

A Dream of Blood

A Dream of Wolves

A Dream of Stone

A Dream of Ravens

A Dream of Bones

www.ingramcontent.com/pod-product-compliance
Lightning Source LLC
Chambersburg PA
CBHW030801190726
48285CB00003B/972